Never through Miami

Never through Miami

Roberto Quesada

Translated from the Spanish by
Patricia J. Duncan

Arte Público Press
Houston, Texas

This volume is made possible through grants from the City of Houston through The Cultural Arts Council of Houston, Harris County.

Recovering the past, creating the future

Arte Público Press
University of Houston
452 Cullen Performance Hall
Houston, Texas 77204-2004

Cover design by Giovanni Mora
Cover art courtesy of Alejandro Romero

Quesada, Roberto.
   [Nunca entres por Miami. English]
   Never through Miami / Roberto Quesada; translated from the Spanish by Patricia J. Duncan.
       p.   cm.
   ISBN 1-55885-366-9 (trade pbk. : alk. paper)
   I. Duncan, Patricia J. II. Title.
PQ7509.2.Q44 N86 2002
863'.64—dc21   2001056720
                                                                       CIP

2 3 4 5 6 7 8 9 0 1   10 9 8 7 6 5 4 3 2 1

A city . . . was not merely a pile of bricks and mortar, peopled by a certain number of inhabitants; it was a thing with a soul characteristic and distinct; an individual conglomeration of life, with its own peculiar essence, flavour and feeling.

O. Henry, *The Making of a New Yorker*

This book is dedicated to the world's immigrants who, successfully or unsuccessfully, have abandoned what they love and ventured in search of their Personal History for the well being of those they love and for themselves. To all, for being courageous.

Sometimes it is impossible to stop the river of life.

Paulo Coelho, *The Alchemist*

Miami International Airport

Control, control, control. Yes, that's the word that will save me. Words save; words are divine; they can rescue you. But sometimes they can do you in, too. Speak little, only what you must, or not at all. Silence is not as wise as people think; sometimes an opportune word trumps silence. I can't look nervous. This is the final test, the decisive one, the final door into the United States. That line is long. So many people! How many will get in? Will we get in? How many will be detained? How many deported? Being here is like *to be or not to be*. I have to practice my English mentally. The little bit that I know can save me. Once again, words can save me but this time in another language. Which language's words are more important? I have to concentrate on practicing while the line is moving; I must practice my pronunciation because if I say *two beer or not two beer*, they will probably deny me entry for being drunk. My documents are in order, my visa is valid, I look like the person in the photograph—yes, it's me, this is me. Nothing is fake, everything is legal. Legal, that is the word that saves. More than anything I am worried about this damned line. "Possession of this visa does not guarantee entry to the United States." What reason would they have for not letting me enter? Documents in order, a letter of invitation. I have no criminal record in my country or any other one. The most important thing is

that I be apolitical and not apocalyptical. Helena will be overjoyed when I tell her I was in Miami. Her beloved Miami.
What is it about Miami that makes so many fall in love with it?
It must be pretty. It's a pity I'm only in the airport, but they say
the best place for an artist is New York. I'll soon see New York.
They say that the most difficult part is this: passing through
customs. Everything is in order. I'm not bringing in any avo-
cados or chickens or dogs or butter or cardboard boxes or anything that is not allowed. Will those two sculptures in my suitcase be a problem? No, they are mine; it's art. Art should get
through without any problem because this is a developed country where they say art is respected. Yes, I think I meet all the
requirements of those who enter with their heads held high.
Here I go . . . It's my turn. Damn, I got that mean one with the
scowl. Be quiet, mind, and stop thinking that here, they have
technology that can read your mind and, *adiós*, New York.
Deported for saying "scowl" in your mind about an immigration officer.

"How long do you plan to stay in America?" the immigration officer asked without looking at him.

He hesitated before that annoyed face. How could that fat
little woman with glasses and the snout of a Pekinese, who was
studying the photo like an x-ray, have more power than he? The
freckled little midget looked up and glared into his eyes, urging him for a response. He managed to say, "I'm sorry. No
English."

She looked at the passport from back to front, page by
page, as if looking for the *corpus delicti,* and then she translated her question.

"*¿Cuánto tiempo piensa quedar en América?*"

He wanted to respond with the lyrics of a romantic Latin

song, "My whole life I would spend with you," but that intimidating freckled face was there fulfilling its purpose of terrifying the new arrivals. He knew he had to say a number of months, and the maximum for his visa was six; there was no minimum. Saying six might be cause to deport him. How will you earn a living all that time? Saying less—two weeks, for example—could mean laying his own trap, for they would stamp his passport for two weeks and he would have to leave on that day or sink to the miserable status of an illegal, something he had never even considered.

"Six months."

"*¿Cuál ser la razón de su viaje?*"

"To visit my family?" He said as quickly as possible so she wouldn't understand and wouldn't ask the next question: "What family do you have here?"

What could I say? I had no one here. I would have to say my great big family, all the Gonzálezes, Pérezes, Lópezes, Martinezes, Ruizes, Fernándezes . . . my great big Latin American family. Fortunately, the officer was more interested in concrete things than in what family I had here.

"*Mostrarme su boleta para regresar a su país.*"

"I don't have a return ticket. My family will buy it for me when it's time for me to go back."

She closed the passport like a door through which the stamp he needed would never enter.

"*Nadie puede entrar a América sin su boleta de* round-trip."

"Without what?"

"*Sin boleta para regresar a su país.*"

He had to help himself somehow, try to convince her or convince himself that dogs are man's best friends, and use his eyes to talk to that Pekinese-faced woman to get her to sympathize with him.

"I didn't buy one because I don't know the exact date I will return. I may stay less than I thought, or maybe I'll buy a car and leave by land."

The officer opened the passport. Elías felt that same feeling he felt when Helena had refused for so long to open her legs and then, without any warning, opened them like an invitation. But the two situations were very different. In Helena's case, he had the advantage of being owner and lord of the stamp, while the officer had left him without doors and without stamps, and worse yet, without keys. The officer examined the passport page by page, even more scrupulously than before. He felt the blow on his face of every door that was opened, the infinite passport, as long as a novel before the age of television.

"*¿Haber estado en América?*" the officer asked in broken Spanish and her legs open.

"Yes, I have," he replied hurriedly, before the hinges announced another slam of the door.

"*¿Cuántas veces?*"

"Three times."

She looked at the wide-open passport.

"*Aquí no dice.*"

"That passport is new."

"*Mostrarme su pasaporte anterior.*"

"I left my old passport in my country."

The officer placed her index finger between her legs and closed the door halfway. Elías was sweating, and he felt the stamp would never fit through such a tiny opening.

"It doesn't show here that you have been in America. Here it shows that it's your first time. We need your old passport.

¿En qué trabajar usted?"

"*Soy escultor*," he said almost proudly, under the illusion that the magic of art would also be useful for passing through customs.

She was pensive and appeared to be thinking over the word so it would come out perfectly.

"*¿Escalator?*" she said in English. "Odd job, I don't know what an *escalator* is exactly."

Elías was losing hope; he could not let the door close, leaving him outside. He gestured and used body language.

"*Soy escultor*," and just as the agent was removing her finger from the middle of the passport, with just a sliver of light coming through the door, something brilliant came to him. "I am Leonardo da Vinci."

For the first time the passport-checking machine had a human reaction; she was surprised. "*¿Sentirse usted bien?*"

Sweating as if untangling a spider web from his face, Elías said, "No, no, I'm not da Vinci . . . I have the same job."

Then, having understood, she took off the human mask and returned to her normal state.

"Oh, yes, I see, *comprende . . . escultor.* Wait here," and she removed her finger from between her legs and closed the passport with a blow that hit Elías in the face. Dejected now and trying to invent some heroic reason to explain to his family, friends, and enemies why he was deported, he headed for the room the midget woman indicated to him, to wait, along with all the others, for the final judgment.

Just as he had found the peace that comes from resignation and was close to finding that empty space we all need to escape from reality and plunge into sleep's refuge, he heard his name in the distance, as if his soul were being called from Purgatory. His name resonated in his eardrums, weak, transparent, and elastic. It fell on his ears slowly, letter by letter, as if released from a dropper. E l í a s S a n d o v a l. It couldn't be him they were calling because the other Elías who had recently left his country was full of optimism and dreams of triumph. It was a name made of stainless steel. They brought him back from his refuge as if he were dreaming and passing through customs by way of another dimension, where documents were not needed. He woke up completely, and in a fraction of a second his mind was clear: the airport in Miami, the long wait, and now getting up from his seat to come face to face with another officer. Something told him it was worth giving it another try with the new officer because he saw a very different person from the small-faced Pekinese woman. This was a stylish, very good-looking man who carried himself in the manner of those who are proud of their features, their bodies and their inner selves do.

"How long do you plan to stay?" the officer asked in perfect Spanish.

Elías felt the relief that comes with being abroad and all of a sudden hearing someone speak your language.

"Six months."

"How much money do you have?"

"A thousand dollars."

"That's not much for six months."

"I have family in New York, a place to stay and meals. I won't have other expenses, and besides . . . ."

"Show me the thousand dollars."

Elías had not anticipated an interrogation of his finances, but, fortunately, he had a response handy that he felt was satisfactory.

"I spent some of it in the airport in my country in the duty-free shops. I bought gifts for my family in New York."

"How much money do you have, then?"

"Not quite five hundred."

"Show me what you have."

He felt the final door coming down on him like a tombstone. He decided to end the lying and his trip.

"The truth is, I'm a sculptor. One of my sculptures was bought in New York, and I'm going to be paid for it when I get there. Right now I only have eighty dollars."

The officer blew a little air out of his mouth, as if he was about to whistle, and he shook his head from side to side.

"With eighty dollars you can't last a single night in New York."

"I have family in. . . ."

"Go sit down. We'll talk when it's your turn."

"I think I missed my flight."

"I can only give you a visa for one day."

"I don't want one day. I'd rather be sent back to my country."

"Go sit down."

An hour went by, the longest hour of his life. Elías found himself in the tunnel that connects life with death. It was a tunnel with a life of its own; it could be longer than you could possibly imagine or so short that you could pass through it in less than a second. Whoever found himself in that tunnel did not fear either end but rather the tunnel itself. Desperation led to escape through the closer of the two exits. If you were closer to the death end, you would beg, because the doctor of death might feel sorry for you and administer euthanasia. But if you were near the other end, you would ask God not to take you yet, to give you a little more time to settle your affairs.

Elías was in the worst part of the tunnel—the middle. From there he sat up and shouted, "Are you going to send me back to my country or am I going to see my family? I missed one flight and I'm going to miss another. What have I done to be kept here like this? I'm not a murderer, I'm not a thief; I'm just an artist. I can't believe this is happening. You send whomever you want to my country. We've let you install more than twenty military bases. Three airports were built for you and your wars. We protect you from the Commies . . . and me, a harmless artist, can't enter your country. Where is that famous democracy?"

The officer interrupted his speech. "All right, calm down, we're seeing what we can do for you. Your case is sensitive," he said as he patted Elías a couple of times on the shoulder with an expression meant to comfort him. Then he signaled for him to follow, and they went into a cubicle. The officer sat down in front of a computer and offered him the seat across from him.

"Our country always gives preferential treatment to artists, but, of course, the artists I'm talking about are those who have already distinguished themselves in other countries, those who have respected résumés, those who stand above the rest. Can you imagine if that preferential treatment were given to all artists indiscriminately? The country isn't big enough for all the artists in the world who want to live here."

"Yes, I know. And I also know that others whose work is very good and important have been denied entry."

"Of course, it has to be that way. If you spotted an enemy of yours trying to enter your house, would you let him in?"

"No."

"Well, it's the same with countries, only your case isn't

political. It's a matter of law: You can't enter the country without a return ticket."

Hoping that the officer would forget about the matter of the ticket, Elías asked naively, "You're Cuban, right?"

The officer, who was inspecting the passport, looked at him from over his eyeglasses. "Cuban-American."

"It was a tragedy what happened in Cuba."

The officer feigned surprise. "What tragedy? Was there a hurricane or an earthquake?"

"No, the political situation. What happened with the Russians . . . "

"I am apolitical."

"But this is about your country."

"It's not my country. I've never been there; I don't know it at all. I was born here. It may be my parents' country, but it's not mine."

"But your Spanish is so good."

"Naturally, my parents are educated people. I speak Castilian Spanish like they do."

"Your parents must have suffered a great deal to get out."

"Suffered? Not my parents. My grandparents maybe, especially my grandmother. She married my grandfather when she was very young, and ever since elementary school when she found out that Cuba was an island, she was unable to live in peace. It got worse as she got older. The idea of living in a place surrounded by water tormented her. That was why my grandfather, as soon as the economic situation permitted, had to leave the island, and Miami was the closest place. My grandmother liked Miami, but she would have liked any place that wasn't an island."

"I thought it was because of politics . . . ."

"Your passport doesn't show that you have been in this country before."

"But I have, believe me, three times."

"Where?"

"In New Orleans."

"Doing what?"

"Showing my work."

"It doesn't show that here."

"But it does in my old passport."

"It's too bad you didn't bring it . . . maybe then you would have been able to enter."

"This is unbelievable."

"What is unbelievable?"

"That you send thousands of soldiers to our country and have military bases and airports there, and an artist can't come into yours."

"It's not a question of politics, it's the law. Besides, you asked us to send the Marines."

"Who? I didn't."

"Your government."

"I am apolitical."

The officer looked at him as if giving him one last chance. "Show me the eighty dollars."

"It's sixty, actually."

The officer shook his head from side to side. "That's nothing."

"It's hard to get dollars in my country, but I'm going to be paid two thousand dollars for a sculpture in New York. Really."

"By whom?"

"My fellow countrymen in New York."

"What kind of sculpture?"

"A bust. A bust of Francisco Morazán."

"Who's that?"

"He's a Central American hero from the last century who fought for the unity of Central America, as a single nation that would be great and powerful."

"That's political."

"No, it's my job."

"But it's political. Politics are always involved."

"Not with me. Today I might do Morazán, but tomorrow if they ask me to do a bust of Hitler, I'd do that, too, as long as they pay me, of course."

"There's nothing wrong with being apolitical and doing what you have to, to earn a living, but you shouldn't be so cynical. This country fought against Hitler. Did you bring any sample of your work?"

"In my suitcases . . . Photos . . ."

Elías pulled a small album out of his carry-on bag. "This is the Morazán."

"Looks like mostly busts."

"That's what they want in my country. Everyone wants to have a bust of his own."

"It's not like that in New York."

"I also have another kind of . . . ."

"Yes, it's too bad you didn't bring your old passport," the officer said, unconvinced.

Elías sensed that the door was opening by the magic of an unexpected key, which could well have been the officer's affinity for artists or the simple desire to let him in.

"Look me up in the computer. I have to be there."

The officer looked as if he was about to enter his name but then changed his mind and took off his glasses. "I'll let you in.

But don't come again without a return ticket."

"I missed my flight."

"Go to the airline office and they can resolve that."

"Thank you."

"How long do you want me to give you?"

Elías hesitated. "Six months."

The door was wide open, and the stamp was about to come smashing down. For Elías the moment was never-ending. He remembered Helena's legs and his triumphant entrance. The officer returned his passport.

"Good luck in New York."

"Thank you, thank you very much."

Queens, New York, Two Weeks Later

After two weeks in New York, he was like a puppy that can't even imagine opening its eyes one day. He needed everything—a mouth to speak another language, eyes to take it all in, ears to distinguish which noise came from what, amid so much noise, and courage to handle the fear that sometimes appears like the prelude to a storm. Mario opened up a subway map, and Elías was lost in that labyrinth of lines, letters, numbers, a hodgepodge of hieroglyphics. It was unthinkable that one day he might learn to get around by himself. He felt like a little boy learning to walk, who takes two little steps, laughs, loses his balance, and, just when he's about to fall, two grownup arms appear to save him and congratulate him. He was that little boy but without those grownup arms, a grownup forced to behave like a little boy.

"It's your second week in New York. So what do you think?" Mario asked him as he hung the map on the wall so he could look at it every day and familiarize himself with the essential routes for getting around the city.

"It's incredible. I'm a little afraid, though."

"That's normal in the beginning. You'll get used to it."

"I have ten dollars left," Elías said meekly, ashamed, knowing that that was nothing, that it would barely buy a couple of slices of pizza and a drink.

"You have to find a job. Let me talk to my friends."

"Yeah, I need to find a job and to meet people in the art world. I have to show my work. After what I went through in Miami to get into this country, it better not be for nothing."

"What you went through? Stop exaggerating. What you told me is hardly an ordeal. Didn't you say the second officer was nice?"

"But he humiliated me."

"Oh, come on, I don't believe that."

"Sure he did: he gave me a lesson on artistic ethics. He told me not to be cynical by saying that today I could do a Morazán and tomorrow a Hitler."

"Why did you say that?"

"Capitalism. I thought I'd surprise him by showing my love of money."

"You're pretty naïve. You forgot he was Cuban. Even against their will, they have Martí in their veins."

"And Fidel."

Mario let out a laugh. "Don't even joke about that. That would be the worst reason for your being deported. The officer was clever, eh? That's what happens when you underestimate people. The ignorant one was you."

"I know, but that's no reason to laugh," Elías muttered, smiling sadly.

"Not for you, of course, but for me and others who might hear it, it is. It's no wonder: the learned sculptor was crushed by an immigration officer. This time by sheer force of intelligence."

Elías picked up the remote control and turned the television on. "Maybe it was because he didn't believe anything you said, except that you were an artist. He must have said to himself, with all the undocumented illiterates there are, one more won't make a difference, and at least this one knows how to read."

Mario laughed, but Elías failed to see what was so funny.

"Yeah, but I paid a price. I suffered."

Mario lifted his head up from the bed and watched the television as Elías flipped through the soundless channels and then said, "That's not suffering. Imagine the people who are beaten up at the borders or those who are eaten by sharks, or those who are in jail with families who know nothing about them."

Elías put down the remote control, leaving the television on, and looked straight into Mario's eyes. "My suffering is just as great as theirs."

Mario plopped down on the bed. "Please! Have a little more respect for the victims!"

"It's different. People who endure things like that are uneducated illiterates who can survive only by brute force. So it is unfair that one should have to endure the same things they do. Our suffering is greater because small things hurt us."

Mario was speechless. Finally, he said, "Ask Hitler if there were differences between educated and non-educated Jews. Ask Mao if there was a difference between a rice farmer and an intellectual. You know what? Don't ever do a Morazán or a Bolívar again, or anyone like that. Devote yourself to a series of Hitlers. If I had been the immigration officer, not only would I not have let you in, I would have thrown you in jail."

Elías shot him a condescending look. "Yeah, yeah, it's just

a conversation. You give the example of the Jews suffering, and look what happened. Now they are in control in this country, and what? They forgot all about what they went through. Now they want to do exactly what Hitler did to them. There is no evolution. What they did to you yesterday, you'll do to someone else tomorrow."

"Stop exaggerating. The immigration situation today is not the same as Hitler's genocide."

"But it is the same. It's just a question of letting things continue as they are, and you'll see that the only thing that's changed are the tactics, the strategy, how it gets done. In the end, it's the same. The short little woman was a nightmare. But I have to admit that the Cuban-American officer was nice."

"Okay, but don't call it suffering."

"What else could it be?"

"I have faith that New York will teach you how to suffer."

"Are you wishing me bad luck?"

"No, but you shouldn't compare what happened to you with what happens to people who are really humiliated and abused when they are captured or deported."

"Whose fault is that? Look at Mexico, such a big, rich country, and it allows its sons to be beaten and humiliated for crossing the border in search of a bite to eat. The corrupt governments we have had and still have in our countries are also to blame. There is no national conscience. As for suffering, I don't disagree with you, but I do believe that intellectual suffering is just as bad, if not worse, than physical suffering."

"I'll give you that one from a philosophical standpoint, but this isn't the time to talk about philosophy. You shouldn't complain. You were lucky. One lie is enough to send you back."

"You're scaring me. I don't know why the idea of going back scares me."

"Were things so bad there?"

"It's not that. Some people are just born in the wrong countries. Just look at how some who are born in big cities go off to live in the countryside or in small countries and stay there for the rest of their lives. Other people are just the opposite. I know making a living as an artist is difficult anywhere, even though you are living proof that you can live . . . ."

"Don't believe everything you see. I work part-time in a lab. I photograph weddings and birthday parties on weekends. Get it? I also shoot for a small newspaper on Long Island, and when I have time, I do what I like to do: artistic photography."

"Yeah, I get it. But even that is impossible there."

"Of course, here is still better than there."

"I'm going to succeed, too. I'm going to get in touch with people in the art world, look for a job, and bring Helena over."

"I was surprised you hadn't mentioned her tonight."

"She's so beautiful. She made me believe in love."

"You're not going to get all mushy on me, are you? It embarrasses me because I, too, felt the same way once. We Latinos are unpredictable. At a certain age we are terribly romantic, and then we get over it and become complete cynics, Don Juans."

Elías wasn't listening. "I'll bring her over as soon as I can."

"That sounds good, but it's not so easy."

Elías unzipped his sleeping bag and got inside. "Lots of men have brought their wives over."

"And lots have left them for good. Without even a letter."

"Yeah," he said, yawning, " I know of one case."

"There's more than one," Mario said, wrapping himself up in the sheet. "Does Helena want to come?"

"Of course, she does. That's how we left it. She dreams of living in the United States, even though she has never left the country."

"You have to get settled first."

"Is it possible to do something here with my sculpture?"

"Here, anything is possible. You just need talent and luck. It's not hard to meet people in the art world—Latinos, that is. You should try to break into that world first; then later you can try to break into the Anglo market. Better yet, ask Botero." Mario settled into his bed, a sign that sleep was overcoming him.

"I know you don't want to scare me. That's why you're making it sound so easy."

"No one said it was easy, but no one said it was impossible, either. I'll help you any way I can, and one way is to tell you my secret: Don't give up. In order to live here in New York or anywhere in the world, for that matter, you need to dream. Dream that you are going to be someone, and until it happens, dream it and enjoy it. For example, I dream about magazines like *Life, Time, Art News,* or the prestigious European magazines. Even though I know it may never happen, as long as I dream, I can enjoy it, and while I am enjoying it, I work so that the chance that it might happen increases. But if it doesn't happen, I'll have spent seventy years dreaming, and I'll die happy, like in a dream."

Elías stared at the subway map on the wall. "If Helena is with me, I can dream. I have to bring her here."

"You're saying that because you just got here. Later you'll

end up marrying for a green card."

"What *gringa?*"

"Not *gringa,* green card."

Elías, also succumbing to sleep, smiled, and, as if to himself said, "Who could that *griiin—ga* be?"

Mario's voice came from the portals of sleep. "It's your turn to turn off the light."

"I don't mind sleeping with the light on."

Mario's fading words came when darkness had already come. "Don't be so lazy . . . ."

The Songbird

She sings in the shower, after the shower, in the bedroom, in the living room, and on the balcony. She sings all the time, and when someone sings, it is for one of two reasons: having just arrived or wanting to leave. Except for when she came into the world, she had never just arrived anywhere, so she could only sing because she wanted to leave. People usually left with singing. The person in prison knows he can escape as far as his singing can go. If the song passes through the bars, he is no longer in prison but wherever his song is. Those who have just arrived sing another kind of song, the song that hopes to reach what they left behind, the song that in some way brings them closer to what they don't want to drift away from. But there are also ambiguous songs, like Helena's. It had the strength of one who wants to leave, but at the same time, it left a resounding echo for what it was leaving behind—in this case, her *mamá*. She desperately wanted to follow Elías, but when she took his side mentally, she despaired and suddenly sided with her mother. Then, when she closed her eyes and thought about one and then the other, her life became a turmoil of continuous jumping back and forth, which is why she was frightened when she began to fall asleep. When she sang, subconsciously, the two things she was jumping between came together, and she no longer needed to jump to be everywhere or, at least, to be in the two places she wanted to be: with her husband and with her mother, and in that order, because that was the order she had in her mind when she wanted to feel that feeling of being with one and without the other.

Helena got out of the bath with her towel around her head, like she had seen in magazines. She liked the idea of looking like someone in a magazine more than someone in a movie. She didn't like people in movies because they disappeared, when the movie ended, and wound up on a roll of film, while people in magazines were always there; even when the magazine was closed, they were within reach. She stopped in front of the mirror in the living room and inspected her eyebrows as she sang. She examined them so closely that one would have thought she was counting the hairs, as if preparing for a radio contest of ridiculous questions: How many little hairs are in your eyebrows?

Then the telephone interrupted her, and her singing was shattered by a brief silence of doubt and emotion. Finally, she answered the phone, and it was just the call she had been waiting for. Intuition told her so; she didn't have to hear the voice. She was smart enough to realize that the pause, and then the click was the sound of a long-distance call. There was another pause, and then the voice that she had hoped for was saying hello. It was the voice from area code 718 reaching her area code 504. Her emotions kept her from responding immediately. She, too—just like telephones—needed a pause. She heard the voice from area code 504 again, and finally, from her end, came a response.

504: Elías, what a surprise! Darling, I thought you were never going to call.
718: Helena, Helenita my love, it sounds like you're right here next to me.

504: I had a feeling you would call today.

718: I didn't call you before because I didn't have a job. But now I can pay for the call.

504: I thought you might be having some problems.

718: Yeah, I thought you'd understand.

504: Where are you working and why are you using the familiar *tú* form with me?

718: I'm working in a restaurant, but it's temporary, just until I become a famous sculptor.

504: Is it hard?

718: No, not at all. It's fine. You meet a lot of people.

504: How was your trip? Did you have any problems?

718: No, not a one, everything was . . . .

504: And did you have a chance to see Miami?

718: No, we were only there for a little while.

504: Oh, what a shame. It must be sad to pass through Miami and not be able to stay, even for just a day.

718: Well, I was there about six hours.

504: Then you can say you were in Miami.

718: Yeah, it's very nice. It's a very nice city.

504: When I come to meet you, I'm going to make sure I see Miami, even if it's only for a day.

718: No! You won't be coming through Miami.

504: Why are you using the *tú* form with me?

718: I'm telling you that you won't be coming through Miami.

504: I-won't-be-coming-through-Miami? You're crazy. Okay, fine, I'll just stay here, then.

718: You'll come on a direct flight to New York. You'll see how big and beautiful New York is. There are so many nice things. It's much better than Miami.

504: That's impossible. There's nothing like Miami.

718: I'm going to make sure you never come through Miami!

504: Stop using the *tú* form with me!

718: You are not coming through Miami.

504: Then you may as well send for your grandmother.

Helena slammed down area code 504 as if wanting to destroy 718.

* * *

When Helena's mother heard the receiver slam down, she came out of her bedroom to see what had happened. Helena was curled up on the sofa, sobbing uncontrollably, abandoned like the film of a movie that she never wanted to see again.

"What's wrong, *hijita?*"

"He's so rude," was all she said. Her mother looked around, picked up the receiver, and put it to her ear, as if calls never ended. She sat down next to her daughter. "Who are you talking about?"

"Elías. He's horrible."

"He called! It was Elías who called?"

Helena, her voice faltering, managed the difficult task of saying yes.

"What did he say?" her mother asked as she stroked her hair. "It can't be so bad."

"He addressed me using *tú.*"

Her mother jumped. Horrified, she brought her hands to her mouth, and her question filtered through her fingers.

"What? He said *tu madre*, the louse!"

Helena smiled through her tears like someone swimming against the current.

"No, just with *tú*. He used the familiar *tú* form to address me; he didn't use *vos.*"

The woman regained her breath. "*Ay*, Helenita, that's nothing."

Helena sat down and leaned on her mother's shoulder. "Of course it is; it makes me feel so far away."

"But darling, five thousand miles is far away."

"No, I mean far away in my heart."

"I don't believe that. He loves you."

"So who is teaching him to use *tú*? Could it be some Venezuelan girl? They're famous for . . ."

Her mother picked her daughter's head up off her shoulder. "Now, stop talking about people you don't know."

She began to sob again, and again she found her mother's shoulder. "Then why did he use *tú* with me?"

"You have to understand, darling, society forces him to. Probably when he uses *vos* no one understands him. So he has to use *tú*. He must have his reasons. Maybe if they hear him using *vos*, he runs the risk of being mistaken for an Argentine."

"In that case, Elías would be right. On the TV, I saw that they wanted to kill an Argentine. I wonder why."

"Because they say they think they are the best in the world," the mother said, downplaying the importance of her statement.

Helena lifted her head from her mother's shoulder. Only traces of her tears remained.

"That shouldn't be a crime. Everyone should have the right to believe whatever they want, even the Argentines. I don't think it's that. I think it's that beautiful *zho* they have, the way they say it, drag it, *Zho crezho que hoy va a zhover, piba.* That's it, jealousy of the Argentine *zho*."

The ring of the telephone pierced the dialogue, and Helena went to pick it up, saying, "It's for me."

504: Darling, I'm sorry. I knew you were going to call. I spoke with my mother, and she explained everything to me, and now I understand."

718: Thank heavens she didn't take your side. I'm surprised and glad.

The mother looked as if she were about to leave the room and leave them alone, but Helena signaled her to stop.

504: Of course, they might think you are Argentine.

718: What are you talking about?

504: Your addressing me with *tú*. I won't get mad ever again.

718: I'm sorry, but I thought we were talking about my telling you not to come through Miami.

504: What? You're crazy! That's not even up for discussion! Me not going through Miami? Not likely!

718: Look, I'm going to tell you what happened to me.

504: What do you mean what happened to you? You're just selfish. You want to know more than I do.

718: No, Helena, that's not it. It's dangerous to come through Miami.

Helena's fake burst of laughter frightened her mother.

504: Do you think you're talking to a fool? Miami dangerous? That is the first time I've heard anyone say such a stupid thing.

718: Darling, listen to me, don't come through Miami.

504: I asked you not to use *tú* with me.

718: You have to believe me, Helena, don't come through Miami.

504: I asked you not to address me with *tú*.

718: I'm not.

504: Yes, but that *vos* you're using is not the Argentine one. And the Argentine one is the one I like.

And 504 again slammed down furiously on 718, who had no chance to be heard.

The mother had a feeling from the one side of the conversation she heard that the problem was not exactly the Argentine use of *vos*. However, she used it as a lure so that Helena would reveal the half of the conversation she had not been privy to.

"*Hija*, don't make him say things you shouldn't. You'll see when you go there. You'll also be using *tú* with me."

"Or, in the worst case, he'll use the Argentine *vos*."

"Then put yourself in his shoes and try to understand him."

Helena removed the towel from her head and went over to the mirror. "Fine, let him use the familiar form with me. I'm going to feel like Miss Venezuela."

"You should use it with him, too, so you get used to it."

"Uh-huh," she said, removing a hairpin she was holding in her lips. "I think the most important language in New York is the Puerto Rican *tú* form, the Dominican *tú*, the Cuban *tú*, the South American *tú*, and then, as a third language, English."

"That's very smart, *hija*. The first language is the one you use to communicate with your own people."

"Yeah, but that's not the problem," and she stressed the last word as she continued combing her hair in front of the mirror. The mother acted surprised. "What happened? Did he mention another woman?"

"No, nothing like that. I trust him."

"Are you pregnant?"

Helena turned around to face her mother and placed her hand down over her belly button, pointing out her slim figure. "How long has it been since Elías left? It would show by now, wouldn't it? And it's impossible over the phone."

"With today's technology you never know," the mother

mumbled.

"What?"

"I said, do you think you don't love him anymore?"

"No, Mamá, no. It's something I can't describe, something awful." She took a few steps toward her mother, stopping to dry her hair with the brush, and she went on, "It's the worst thing a human being can do to his spouse. It's unforgivable."

Her mother looked worried and sat down on the couch, as if waiting for the final press release from the President of the United States officially announcing the end of the world. "Trust your mother; you always have."

Despite her efforts, Helena could not contain her crying. "He doesn't want me to go through Miami when I go to meet him in New York."

Her mother jumped up, furious, and more for herself than for Helena she said, "He told you that? The bastard! No, no, Helenita . . . That is unforgivable. How dare he. It's incredible how someone can change so much in only three months!"

Dina the Professor

Dina, Helena's mother, had never been a *doña* or a *señora* because she forbade anyone to age her prematurely or to call her anything other than her name. That is the main reason she became a professor (she was really a grammar school teacher, but in her country, anyone who taught was called professor). She allowed people to call her professor since it was a neutral word in terms of age; there were as many young professors as old ones. That was why she was most thankful for having studied: so she could be called professor. On the other hand, what would *doña* or *señora* reveal? She had to put up with it without complaint as many did. Dina was 'Dina' to her friends and 'professor' to everyone else. She was still young, and getting older might not have bothered her so much except for the fact that she had not realized her greatest dream: to see Miami.

She found Miami by chance, or rather, Miami found her, because she had never left her country. She had access to magazines, TV shows, videos, and it was thanks to her school that Professor Dina became an expert on Miami without ever having left the country. Without intending to, she had humiliated more than one lady from the ministry or some other random person because the important subject of Miami would come up suddenly and no one could talk about it the way she could: she knew the streets, the buildings, the psychological traits of the people, the jewelry stores, the beaches, and the hotels. You could tour Miami step by step with her. She even knew the exact location of the houses of the Latin American pop stars and television producers.

Even so, she did not lose hope. She put it into her husband's head that he should go to Miami to work and then he could send for her and their little girl Helena. Convincing her husband was not easy. Not even as a joke had such a crazy idea like breaking up his family occurred to him. Dina almost forced him, offering examples of others who had done so and throwing her physical attributes in his face, attributes that could have earned her an upper-class husband. She had been faithful, although more than once she had been tempted, thinking about those vacations in Miami that had been proposed to her on a couple of occasions. But she had passed them by, not because of her husband but because of her fervent religious faith. Finally, her husband had no choice: His life had become the path to Golgotha, literally, since she deliberately removed the springs in his mattress and replaced them with pointed wires so that when he went to take a nap after a brutal day of work, he leapt out of bed with a terrible scream. She usually took advantage of that moment to tell him how well they would live if he would stop being so foolish and just go to Miami. His daughter didn't pay any attention to him, either. Through her mother's stories, Helena had grown accustomed to seeing Miami from afar. The husband left for Miami, but he never contacted her again; the curse of Perestroika had fallen on her, deservedly.

Despite all of her setbacks, Dina was prepared to fight until the end. She didn't care how roundabout her route to Miami would be, how long she would have to wait, or the strategies she would have to employ. Helena was one of her last cards to play to undo Perestroika once and for all.

Waiters and Waitresses in Transit

What did it mean to work as a busboy in his country? He had to forget that question. In Latin America, the job speaks for the person: an ordinary bank employee, though he may earn a pittance, is above a bricklayer or a waiter, who may earn more. Life isn't measured in real terms of how much someone has but in superficial ways, like who looks more impressive than the others. Jobs can even cause arguments. A mother might scold her daughter saying that she will wind up marrying a carpenter. The daughter might be so offended that, in order to get revenge and show her mother she was wrong, might go to bed with a carpenter several times and then forget him, as if nothing had ever happened. The carpenter knows this and enjoys talking about the adventure every time he gets together with his buddies. The story will be told over and over again, and each time the carpenter practically relives the affair. The girl will try to forget it, but she will always avoid looking at construction sites. So the only winner is the carpenter, because according to his proletarian philosophy, everything good, obtained without having set out for it, is profit, even if only in his memory.

* * *

At first, Elías cursed his job as he cleared the tables, which only made him twice as tired. Exhausted from the nonstop running from one table to the next, and from the embarrassment of feeling inferior, like a slave, he just imagined he was waiting on people who were far below his intellectual level.

That resentment began to fade as he got to know his co-workers. Beautiful waitresses, who were graduates of prestigious universities and who sometimes had more than one degree. Aspiring movies stars, models, painters, you name it. It was the same with the men. When he asked them how they felt about doing that kind of work, they always had an answer on the tip of their tongues, giving the example of some movie star, painter, novelist, or somebody like that who had started out the same way. And so it was that he bought into the common illusion that was held by people in similar circumstances: Everything is transitory; the best, one's true calling, is waiting just around the corner. This was of some use to him, for now he returned to his apartment with only one reason for being exhausted.

Love from Afar

Dina and Helena, immersed in a soap opera, heard the ring and sat up in unison.

"It's him," the daughter said. "I told you he would call back."

"Let me get it," the mother said. Helena agreed.

From area code 504 came a cold voice:

504: Hello.

Area code 718 did not perceive the coldness, and he responded with warmth.

718: Professor Dina, I'm so glad you answered the phone! Helena won't listen to me.

504: What is it that Helena won't listen to?

718: That it's better if she comes on a direct flight without stopping in Miami.

504: Why?

718: In Miami they ask for a lot of things. The immigration officers are more demanding there.

504: Don't be ridiculous, Elías. I wasn't born yesterday. Immigration officers are the same everywhere, even in the movies. If they didn't comply with certain requirements, they wouldn't get those jobs. They have to be that way.

They have to look mean, even though at home they are nice. That's no reason for Helena not to go through Miami. Stop making up stories. How did you get in without any problems?

718: Because I was lucky and got a nice officer.

504: You just contradicted yourself. First, you say that all immigration officers are mean, and now you say you got a nice one.

718: I didn't say they were all mean. You did.

504: Now you're going to accuse me of badmouthing U.S. immigration. I get it. You're doing this so that if my telephone line is tapped, they will open a file on me, and if Helena or I try to go, they won't let us in. I said they look mean, which is not the same as saying they are mean.

718: You have to listen to me, Professor . . . .

504: Anything but that. I won't let my daughter miss out on the dream that I could never fulfill, not when it's so close. She has to go through Miami.

718: New York is beautiful. Besides, from here we can travel to Miami. We could even send for you and all three go together.

The voice from area 504 became more intrigued.

504: Send for me to go to Miami?

718: Sure. Just think, Professor . . . .

Helena went over to area code 504 and managed to half-hear what area code 718 was suggesting. "Don't let him blackmail you, Mamá. Don't let him bribe you. He's trying to trick you."

718: Miami is nice, Professor.

504: No, my daughter will go through Miami or she won't go at all.

Helena took the phone away from her mother and began to yell.

504: So there, you heard it, darling, I'm going through Miami. So don't let the fact that you are there in New York go to your head. It's enough that I've allowed you to address me with *tú*. I'll let you use *tú* with me, but the question of Miami is not negotiable. Since before you left you knew that one of the reasons I wanted to go to the States was to see Miami. If that can't be, then I'm better off staying here.

She slammed area code 504 down as if trying to destroy 718.

* * *

Mario saw Elías's shaken face and became angry. "Did she hang up on you again? If I were you, I wouldn't spend another dollar calling those old broads."

Elías opened the refrigerator and took out two beers. "That's because you don't know what it's like to be in love."

Mario picked up the beer and dried it with a towel. "Well, then let her come any way she wants. Why the hell do you make such a big deal over something that never was? Nothing happened to you. You didn't have a return ticket and what happened to you happens to everyone who doesn't have one. It's the law. That won't change, no matter where you enter."

Elías picked up the can. "Look, even though I might seem like an overly sentimental Latino, I came here motivated by the dream that Helena and I would live here. What sense does it make now if she doesn't come? I can't go back, either, because of what people will say: coming to the land of opportunity and leaving without anything or anybody waiting for me."

"What do you care what they say?" Mario paused to take a drink. "Not everyone who leaves his own country succeeds. But it's your country, and you can go back whenever you want. Besides, from what you told me, it's your mother-in-law-to-be and not Helena who is dying to see Miami. It's Helena you care about; screw the old lady."

Elías smiled. "She's not old. You'd like her."

"Then bring her to me and I'll make her forget all about Miami."

Elías burst out laughing. "Not even as a joke would I accept that challenge. Nobody, not even the best team of psychologists in the world, can make my soon-to-be-mother-in-law give up her dream of visiting Miami before she dies."

"It can't be so important."

"You have to know her."

Two for tú

There had been no singing in the house for days, not even from the radio. The silence in the living room spread to the bedroom, then to the bathroom, and so on throughout the house. When someone spoke, the words took longer to reach the listener's ears since the silence was so loud that the words clashed with it. They had to be pushed out, like when a newborn breaks through a membrane.

The mother, who was the most optimistic of optimists, tried to encourage her daughter to sing again, to motivate her so that her self-esteem would rise to the point of thinking she was the most beautiful of all and that Elías would have to give in sooner than later.

"Listen, Helenita," her mother said.

Helena did not respond because she did not hear; the words barely broke through the membrane of silence.

The mother repeated "Listen, Helenita" so that these words would push the others and finally reach her daughter. The membrane gave way.

"Yes, Mamá."

With her eyes her mother beckoned Helena to sit down next to her, and with the newspaper open, she began to read. "The First Lady returned from a wonderful shopping trip to Miami. Besides doing some Christmas shopping, our First Lady was able to attend concerts of well-known Latin American performers who reside in that great city, known as the capital of Latin America. From her tanned skin we can also assume that the First Lady did not miss the opportunity to enjoy the beautiful, warm beaches. She was welcomed in person by the president at the airport in the capital yesterday at . . . ."

Helena brought her hands to her chest, looked upward with a smile on her face, and, dreaming out loud, said, "I will be in Miami one day too, just like the First Lady."

Her mother looked delighted, closed the newspaper and tossed it aside. "Of course, you will, dear. Then you can invite me to spend some time with you."

"Some time, no, don't even think about it. You will come and live with us. Do you think I could possibly leave you alone? I don't know how I can go even a month without seeing you, Ma. That worries me even now." Helena's happy face turned to one of worry. "Who will make sure that our trip appears in the newspapers here?"

Her mother laughed. "Don't worry, my love, I'll take care of that. I'll take care of everything at this end."

"How wonderful, just imagine the article: Helena and her mother travel to New York . . . ."

Her mother jumped. "New York?"

"Yes, New York. What does it matter? Once we are in the United States, it will be easy to get to Miami. We can even convince Elías that we should live there."

Her mother regained her composure. "Of course, there's no question about that. But don't think about that now."

"About what, Ma?"

Her mother grimaced. "You've forgotten what your father did to us. It's not a good idea for a man to go to Miami by himself."

Helena looked worried, too. "Mamá, who knows? Maybe he's in jail."

"In jail, my foot. I'd believe that if he hadn't called us at first. Men in Miami aren't single for long. Two months is a long time."

"It's the blondes," she said, trying to support her mother.

Her mother, startled, said, "What blondes? It's just the opposite; it happens because there are so many Latinas in Miami."

"But the Latinas are looking for Americans."

"Sure, and there are plenty who like them. The problem is that they can't communicate with each other. They have to sign up for expensive English classes first."

Helena nodded. "I'm beginning to get it."

The mother stood up so she could act out what she was about to say. "If you were in Miami and had three thousand dollars, would you invest it in English classes?"

"Never. First, I would figure out how much it would be with the exchange rate. That's a lot of money, Ma! No, I wouldn't spend it. I'd put it in the bank, even if I married a Latino. Of course, I'd keep it a secret not even he would know."

Her mother smiled. "Now you get it. That's why I'm telling you: Men who have women in their countries should not go to Miami or even to Alaska."

"What does Alaska have to do with Miami, Ma? The climates are so different."

"For that very reason. In Miami there are too many, and in Alaska there's a shortage."

"A shortage?"

"I'm talking about women, Helenita," and she paused. "Look what your papá did: he abandoned us."

"He must be with some Venezuelan woman."

"What do you have against Venezuelan women?"

Helena feigned sad eyes. "Don't forget, Ma, they use *tú* and it drives the fools here crazy."

The mother's laughter filled the room. "Not just them, but also the Puerto Ricans, the Dominicans, the Colombians . . . ."

"Yes, but it's different. The *tú* of the Venezuelan women is more famous. They've made more soap operas and songs with their *tú*."

The mother was pensive. "I hadn't thought of that. Mexico isn't far behind. Their *tú* may even be more famous . . . How many movies, *rancheras* . . ."

"Who knows . . . Maybe Papá . . ."

"Don't mention that alien," her mother interrupted her without anger or resentment.

"I like that, and I admire you because you use nice words to insult him."

"He is your father, after all," she said, lying down on the sofa. "Besides, we are in this position by accident. We belong to a better class than this, and that's why we should leave, so we can recover our status."

The membrane had reappeared, and the daughter heard only herself. "What if I see him in Miami?"

"Good God, I hadn't thought of that!"

"Should I talk to him?"

The mother lowered her voice. "He wouldn't understand you . . . . Now that he's an alien, he probably speaks only English. He's probably forgotten Spanish altogether. That's how those unfaithful Latinos are . . . ."

"It's just as well. That way I can avoid bumping into that Venezuelan girl."

"You're a smart girl," her mother said, caressing her hair.

"Thanks to you, Ma," she said, using the familiar *tú*.

Her mother beamed with happiness.

"That *tú* sounded wonderful!"

"It's not too soon to start practicing."

Her mother hugged her and gave her a kiss. "You're right. Come on, love, we can start preparing for our trip already. Get the remote control and put on an English-language channel on cable TV. But first turn off the light."

They roared with laughter, not caring anymore if the phone rang or not, as Helena searched for the channel, humming a song once again.

Thiς Iς Neѡ Yorҟ Cițy

The restaurant came to be his home away from home, so, at the end of the day, only his body, not his mind, was tired. That restaurant was part of him, especially since they had given him a promotion. He was no longer the one who cleaned the tables for the waiters; now he was a waiter himself. Now the newly hired Mexican would be cleaning the tables for him.

He liked Laura, the Chicana waitress. She was pretty and optimistic. She never gave up hope that a movie director would walk into the restaurant. She would wait on him, and he would be so pleased with her and tell her that she was just the type he was looking for for his new movie. He would give her a card, she would go to the audition, and she would be chosen for the part. Laura liked Elías, too, and on the days when it wasn't so busy at work, she would invite him to go out, as he was still plagued by the shyness typical of a foreigner. Nights when the restaurant would close early, they would stay behind, eating and drinking as they prepared things for the next day. She loved being with him and defending him from the occasional tasteless joke or helping him with his English.

The bartender was thin with long, blond hair and a propensity for alcohol, but he was a good guy who was sometimes misunderstood because of his jokes. At first Elías cursed him

41

under his breath, too, but he got used to him and he would make fun of him and, no matter what, the guy never got angry; you never saw him lose his sense of humor. And then there was Janeth, a Texan who was tall, also blonde, with a gorgeous body.

"All right," the bartender said, and he clapped his hands to get everyone's attention. "Today we deserve a toast. It's on me."

As they moved chairs, folded tablecloths, and cleared the tables, they laughed and spoke with the bartender, whose voice was accompanied by a concert of glasses clinking together, as he too was tidying his bar.

"If that's the case," Laura said, and as always, perhaps to justify her drink despite how artificial it sounded, she lamented her life, "go ahead and pour mine. The usual. I'm tired of waiting for everything in this city."

"This is your city. Weren't you born here?" Janeth asked, and she banged a tray on the table to get the bartender's attention and motioned that he pour a drink for her, too.

"Yeah," Laura said placing a chair on the tabletop, "but it doesn't matter. I started working as a waitress with the hope that some director would rescue me, and look, I feel more like a waitress than an actress."

"You have to be patient. Maybe you're just tired today."

"Yeah, maybe I'm just tired. Especially today. Tomorrow I may see things differently," She went over to the bar and sat down.

"Sure," Janeth replied.

The bartender dried his hands on his apron. "Why is it that

one of you is speaking English and the other Spanish?"

Laura replied hastily, "So that Elías can practice. Free classes."

The bartender looked for Elías, who was struggling to straighten a curtain. With his heavily accented Spanish, he warned, "Be careful, Elías, remember, nothing is free in New York."

"Don't make him even more afraid than he already is," Laura said, and she began to stir the ice in her glass with a little straw.

"I have to practice my Spanish, too," Janeth said in her imperfect Spanish, "because if I don't make it here, maybe I can get a role in a Mexican movie. I need to improve my Spanish, especially now with the Free Trade . . . ."

"*Libre Comercio*, Janeth," Laura corrected her.

"Thanks."

The bartender laughed and continued in his imperfect Spanish, "Elías is also learning English. One word every two months. That's quite a record."

"I wouldn't make fun of him," Laura said. "Your English isn't so good, either."

The bartender, feeling under attack, tried to shift the focus. "Janeth's Spanish isn't so . . ."

"And why are you dragging me into this," Janeth interrupted. "I haven't said a word."

"I know more than one word, maybe a hundred," Elías defended himself as he took a seat at the bar, too.

"Oh, that's great!" the bartender praised him facetiously.

"Stop making fun of him," Laura said, and although she

had never seen Elías's sculptures, not even in photos, she went on, "Elías is a good sculptor, and he needs to learn a little English because he's going to have an exhibition."

"I'm going to help you," Janeth threw in her support.

"Exhibition?" the bartender asked Laura. "He's only been here five months. Did you arrange it for him?"

"That's none of your business," Laura replied.

The bartender laughed playfully. "There's no romance allowed on the job."

Janeth turned to Elías. "Does Mario have a girlfriend?"

"No, he's single."

Laura and Janeth laughed mischievously. Elías liked Laura's laughter and the way she defended him. She had gotten him an exhibition in a small gallery in Soho, which for starters, in New York, was enough. He felt obliged, seduced by such kindness. But the image of Helena limited him to thanking her, and he feigned a shyness uncharacteristic of him, not knowing that it was precisely this quality that made Laura love him even more. It was nice, she thought, to find someone innocent in a city where innocence is more than a sin, it's a crime.

When Laura was close to him, she would rub up against him with those Latin buttocks that had always driven him wild, and he would think how far away Helena was, and that her insistence on coming through Miami had to be a clear sign that she was more interested in Miami than in him, and that with Laura he would have not only an apartment but the famous green card, too. More than anything, he knew she was a woman with whom, were it not for Helena, he could easily fall in love.

"Let's put some music on," Laura said.

"Good idea," the bartender replied, and he quickly did so, adding, "Drink up. I already gave you one on me. Now I'll give you one on the house."

The first to hold out his glass was Elías, something that the bartender, accustomed to taking in many things at the same time, did not let slip by. "Look at the Central American. You guys are all drunks."

"Where do you get off?" Laura blurted out. "What about people from the Caribbean?"

"And Mexicans?" Janeth added.

"And Russians?" Elías did not want to be the only one without an opinion. "And here in this country? This is an alcoholic planet—that's why we were born with a spleen."

The bartender and Laura laughed, while Janeth sat batting her eyelashes, as if that would help her understand the joke. Laura helped her out. "Elías said we were born with a *bazo;* he didn't mean *vaso*," and she raised her glass to illustrate. "He meant the one we have here," and she put her hand on one side of her stomach, over her spleen, "*bazo* is spleen in Spanish, get it?"

Janeth didn't understand but she pretended to, and the others pretended to believe her to avoid further explanations.

"That's another drink on me for Elías's joke," the bartender said. They laughed because the drinks were always on the house and not on the bartender, but in some way they were on him since it was he who managed the bar, therefore he decided. A song by Whitney Houston came on and Laura felt like dancing. She took Elías's hand and they danced in place.

The bartender jumped over the bar and said to Janeth, "We

have to dance, too."

Janeth laughed as if she had begun to feel the effects of the alcohol. Elías held Laura by the waist, and he wished he could hold her naked, just like that, in front of him, close to him, her head resting on his shoulder. Suddenly, he thought of Helena, and for the first time he felt that there was some truth to what Mario had said, that he was too sentimental. That's how he felt, and he knew that for some reason it was stupid to be that way. It was just as silly to be that way as to avoid being that way. Laura suggested they leave and go to her apartment for another drink. He looked for an excuse not to go; he was overcome by an inexplicable fear that if he went with Laura. He would stop loving Helena. He didn't know why he was so afraid of this, just as he didn't know why he was so afraid of falling in love with Laura.

Copy Me

There are people who are real and people who are copies, and there are more copies than real people. At times copies can be so perfect that they are mistaken for the originals. Other times it is difficult to tell the difference between the original and the copy. But, as with anything else, there are methods for detecting copies. If a copy, for example, has a problem, it's not a problem if it knows the formula it copied from the original, but if it doesn't, it avoids looking for a solution to the problem. If the original, on the other hand, knows how to resolve the problem, it does so—and here it is easy to mistake it for a copy—but if it doesn't have the formula to solve the problem, it continues facing the problem, studying it, trying to come up with an analysis that would make it possible to invent a formula that would do away with the problem. The main difference, then, between the original and the copy is that the original thinks and the copy doesn't. Children are copies of their parents until they reach a certain age. Then comes the time when they become aware of their sad role as copies and they rebel against the original, in search of their own freedom not to be a copy of anyone. Adolescence is the stage when who will be a real person and who will be a copy can first be detected. There are copies that cease to be copies of their parents but turn into copies of a friend, or a gang or a lover, in which case they have not ceased to be copies at all but rather have become unfaithful copies. The difference between a faithful and an unfaithful copy is that the unfaithful one deceives his parents by making them believe he has become an original when, just around the corner, for better or worse, there is another original where he returns to his sad role as a copy of another original. It is always danger- ous to be a copy; it is equivalent to being a fanatic member of a cult. Were it not for the proliferation of copies on the planet, Hitler would never have committed genocide, for he would have found no one to follow him. Real people don't follow any- body; only copies do. Without so many copies running around, the odds of war would always be lower, for the masses of sol- diers, those little green copies, ready to seize their weapons whenever their original commanded, would not exist. When all is said and done, copies are the most useless beings that can exist on the face of the earth, for if there were no originals, the copies would never budge from the place they first appeared. Copies long for their originals, for without them they cannot move, and so they become inanimate objects. Helena was a faithful copy of her mother, who in turn was an unfaithful copy of upper-class women.

So it is easy to explain and understand, then, that Helena would know Miami as well as her mother did, just as she had the very same spiritual need to make her dreams of setting foot in what for them was a near copy of paradise come true. If you were to ask them, they would probably say that paradise was a copy of Miami.

There was no step on the stairway of hope for Elías to tread on; Helena would not listen to his petition not to go through Miami. She could easily promise him something that she would not commit to doing. The decision, of course, came from the original, her mamá, another copy, unfortunately, a kind of older copy. The copies were prepared to do everything it took to reach their goal: Miami. Elías, more than a husband or a son-in-law, was being regarded as an airline. They looked at him as they would some worthless being begging for an airline ticket, trying to pass themselves off as community or cultural leaders.

There are both good and bad originals. An example of a good original is Jesus Christ, preacher of the equality of men, who insisted on justice and desired to make us all children of a single God, his Father, who made him superior. Indeed, his original was so good that he did not become jealous when he found out that his father could also be the father of millions. Among the bad originals is Hitler, who also preached equality of men but exterminated those who were not equal. He insisted on justice, but only for those equal to him who were left after the extermination. He, too, had a desire to make us all children of a single god—him.

Elías was neither a good nor a bad original, but at least he had the advantage of not being a copy. He did not have the opportunity to be a good or bad original because he was never a copy, and that is essential to the process. He was not brought up by his parents but by other people, whom he could not imitate because early on he found out that they were not his original. Then he grew up, torn between becoming a copy on some street corner or continuing as a slightly pale original, on the verge of being confused with a copy.

Elías was easily caught in the nets of copies because of his condition of being an eternal original in bloom. A well-made copy can outshine, if only momentarily, a poorly developed original. So the copies set the trap for him of accepting all his conditions, and he swore like a gladiator facing Ceasar—those who will die for you, I salute you—and he decided he would die first if he were not able to get together enough money so that his girlfriend and future mother-in-law could make the trip together.

Mother and daughter were overjoyed, and they sang, and the radio sang. Just the day before, Elías had called for the first time in several weeks, and they laid the groundwork so that what happened with Helena's father, who got lost in paradise, would not happen again.

The mother stopped humming along to the song, lowered the volume on the radio, and spoke to her daughter, who was still singing.

"Tell me what he said to you again. Are you sure you're not making it up, Helenita?"

"Yes, that's what he said."

"How?"

"Just like I told you."

"Tell me again."

Helena stood in front of the mirror and examined her face. "Don't use the *tú* form with me because it might not matter anymore. We probably won't be going anywhere."

The mother replied sternly, "Of course we will; we'll go somehow."

"With what? The dollar is so expensive."

"Somehow. Have faith in your mother. Tell me everything. What a pity I wasn't here. Why are you so happy if he didn't give in?"

"Because there's still a chance. I have the final say. He's going to call tomorrow, and depending on what I say, that's what he'll do."

The mother looked at her slyly. "Are you thinking what I'm thinking?"

Helena smiled. "I think so. If you give up something that you want to do for a few days, while you find the means necessary to get that something, then it's not a sin. Isn't that right, Mamá?"

Darkness

"What was that noise? Was that you, Elías?"

"Uh-huh."

"Aren't you sleepy?"

"Uhh . . ."

"Are you sleepy or not?"

"No, not at all."

"Then why don't you say something instead of just uh-huh uhhhh. That's what you say when you're about to fall asleep or if you don't want to talk to someone."

"Sorry. Yeah, I know. I was just thinking."

"About Helena?"

"Who else?"

"Who knows. You can't tell me you haven't met women at the restaurant. Besides, Laura likes you."

"Uh-huh."

"Either say something or be quiet, but I don't want to hear another uh-huh."

"Wait, I'm starting to come out of my thought. It's very sensitive. I can't just pull myself out of it all at once. That could make me crazy."

"Since you got here, you haven't stopped talking about her, not for one single day."

"I think about how inflexible she is and it bothers me. But I'm thinking more about art."

"What about art?"

"I went to a few sculpture exhibitions with Laura, and it's sad."

"Well, sure. Sculpture is a sad art form because it doesn't move."

"Who says it doesn't move? Of course it does, good sculpture, that is."

"Maybe, but photography has more movement."

"That's nonsense! It depends on who's taking the photograph."

"Yeah, maybe you're right. I've taken photos of some guys that look dead, and I try and help them, retouch them, add light, color, a smile, and they just look worse. Even more dead."

"There are people who seem to be dead, don't you think? I know one."

"Who?"

"You know him, too. My colleague from work, the bartender."

"Yeah, he got tired of trying to become a famous actor and decided to become an alcoholic bartender instead. A novelist was interested in his life and then became disappointed because it was always the same thing: work at the bar, crack jokes, and get drunk. The writer only mentioned him a couple of times. It was an uninteresting life."

"All bartenders are alcoholics."

"But this one more than others, because he's disillusioned."

"Why is it that most of them are actors or actresses?"

"Because the restaurant is located in the Village, where

future movie stars work as waiters and waitresses."

"Life is unfair."

"They have a good time. It's worse for sculptors."

"Why?"

"Because they should be laying bricks to make a living, and that's a life full of sacrifice."

"Does anyone buy sculptures?"

"Of course. If they didn't, there wouldn't be any sculptors."

"The exhibitions I went to with Laura were terrible."

"Why?"

"It was modern art. It's lousy."

"No comment."

"You decorate a piece of junk and it's called a work of art."

"Maybe that's a sign of decadence."

"It is, no doubt about it."

"We may be in a transition period, because all art is decadent."

"Photography?"

"No, photography is an art in evolution, because it's newer. What about theater?"

"I don't know, but it must be faltering."

"Because it's old, it came from the movies . . . ."

"It's different. I wouldn't dare try to label it."

"I'm going to take you to a play and you'll be convinced. Something terrible happens."

"What happens?"

"It's better if you see for yourself."

"But I may not see it. The restaurant's busy these days."

"Well, it's about two guys in a dark room. You don't see anything, you only hear the voices."

"That makes sense. They're about to fall asleep. It sounds good. It's as if you and I were characters in a novel. Any writer who would want to use that dialogue and then try to describe that darkness would have to be an idiot. It's just conversation."

"No, I don't think so."

"Why not?"

"They could be fooling the audience. Maybe there is no scenery, or actors, or anything. Maybe there are just recorded voices."

"Do they turn the lights on at any time?"

"No. It begins and ends that way, in the dark."

"Do they light anything—a match or a lighter to light a cigarette?"

"No, neither of the two smokes. It's a trick. It must be a tape recorder. That way they don't have to pay any actors or a director or anyone to set up the stage, or lighting engineers. They only need two guys: one at the box office and another to turn on the tape recorder and open the curtain."

"What decadence! It's like the sculptures I saw. I could make a million like those."

"That play should be outlawed, or they should make it a radio play: a dark room and two voices."

"Don't they turn the lights on at the end?"

"Yes, but first they close the curtain."

"Don't the actors come out to take a bow?"

"Yes."

"Then, they are real."

"No, because by that time, the box office is closed and the curtain closed. Since it's dark, they may not even open the curtain. The same two guys must be the ones who come out to take a bow. You should see how they applaud."

"How gullible can an audience be!"

"It makes me want to take a flashlight and shine it on the tape recorder. But I'm afraid to, because ruining someone's business here can cost you your life. And the audience could turn on me for having ruined their enjoyment, too."

"What's it about?"

"Two ecologists who can't sleep are arguing that if oil were a different color, it wouldn't harm nature. One defends blue and the other red."

"Who wins?"

"You never find out. Everything is dark, and it seems that one kills the other."

"That's like us."

"But we aren't ecologists and we aren't arguing."

"But I'm afraid."

"Don't worry. A distinguished critic here reviewed the play in *The New York Times*, and he said that the blue ecologist represented the Republicans and the red ecologist the Democrats, even though no one sees the colors. The darkness of the theater is the oil, and the spectators are the little fish, the birds, the plants, all the species that die in the obscurity of the crude oil. The death of one of the ecologists represents the purification of man; humanity is represented there. When one of the two dies, what there wasn't before, now prevails: silence."

"And then what?"

"Nothingness, darkness, silence—that is, death."

"I'm scared. Do you mind if I turn the light on?"

"Yes, I do."

"Stop kidding around."

"It's just a play by two crooks. Ever since the critic's review, that show has played to a full house."

"I'd like that critic to see my exhibition."

"Not likely."

"Today I created a masterpiece."

"Today? In one day? You're crazy!"

"It's not done yet, but almost."

"You're not kidding, are you?"

"Seriously, I've learned that this so-called modern art is easy."

"Let's see, show me, turn on the light."

Let There Be Light

M ario sat down on the bed, his eyes squinting like a vampire exposed to daylight. Elías got out of his sleeping bag and began to rummage through a black bag, from which he pulled a strange object.

"That's junk," Mario said.

"For now, but tomorrow it will be a masterpiece."

"You're not thinking of working at this hour?"

"It won't take any time," he said as he suddenly bent the metal using his foot, took two clothespins and twisted them up in the metal. He tried to give it an incomprehensible shape. He pointed to one side of the object.

"What?" Mario asked, bewildered.

"I'll paint one of these corners green, and there you'll have it."

"Have what?"

"A masterpiece."

"New York is making you crazy."

"You'll see. Maybe I'll paint it blue and red to include both Republicans and Democrats."

"And maybe someone will take offense and knock you over the head with your masterpiece."

"I'll sue him," Elías said, and he sat down on a chair across from Mario and the strange object.

"You're learning how to live in this country."

"Sure, you can't blame me. I'm sticking to the idea that this is my conception of art."

"Elías, I think you should get some sleep."

"I'm not tired."

"Me either, but you're not making any sense. I think you are out of your mind right now."

"I swear to you that to a lot of people this is art."

"It's junk."

"It's art."

"It's the handlebars of an old bicycle. A useless piece of junk."

"It's the new art."

"It's an old bicycle part," Mario said, lying down on his side, his head still propped up on the folded pillow. "Turn off the light."

"No, I'm not turning it off. Not until you tell me you agree with me. It's not good to argue with the lights off. We might end up like those two ecologists. I don't want to be a victim or a murderer."

"You win, it's beautiful! What are you going to call it?"

"Quite simply, *Before the future*."

"Great, or the present, so to speak. You're a genius. Now turn the light off."

"I don't want to talk with the light off."

"All right, as long as you don't talk about that piece of

junk."

"Fine, but first I want to know if you really like the name."

"It's wonderful."

"I like it, too. It's very New York. And now, after that accurate assessment of my masterpiece, it would be a pleasure to oblige you. I'll turn off the light."

"Yes, I think it would be a good idea for you to hold your exhibition in total darkness."

Miami for Beginners

$\int$inging in the dead of night traveled farther, so the mother went into Helena's bedroom and told her to sing only during the day, since the neighbors were sleeping. She stopped singing and assured her mother that only they could hear, for the other houses were a safe distance away, which was true. Her mother knew that, but it was the only excuse she could find for entering her daughter's bedroom. Neither one was sleepy: the younger copy wanted the next day to come so she could talk once and for all to Elías. The older copy couldn't get to sleep because of her curiosity about the conversation her daughter had had with her almost son-in-law the day before.

"Now can you tell me what he said to you?" her mother said, hopefully.

Helena was sitting on her bed, leaning back against the wall. She smiled and said, "It's *puedes,* not *podés*, don't forget we have to practice the *tú* form."

"Oh, yes, how forgetful of me. You're always on top of things. So what did you talk about?"

"What difference does it make? Anyway, I already know how to solve this. I'm going to agree with everything he says, and once I have the ticket in my hands, I'll change it and go through Miami."

"It doesn't matter, tell me," her mother insisted, encouragingly. "If you don't, I'll get angry, and then by the time he calls tomorrow I'll be furious. Then the poor devil will realize he can't play around with my daughter."

Helena was an expert at changing her happy face to a sad one. "He told me that if I didn't agree to go where he thought best, he would cancel the trip, and that I would not go through Miami. Then I said to him: 'Remember, I don't have to do as you say; we're not married.' And you know what he said? 'To hell with marriage, either you come or you don't.' He was shouting, and then he slammed the phone down."

Her mother's eyes opened wide, overwhelming her face, forcing her nose to shift and her mouth to drop open to her chin.

"He's a scoundrel, a *machista*! A wretch! He must have money. Whenever men talk like that, they're hiding something. But where would that good-for-nothing get money if he doesn't know how to do anything?"

"Maybe from his sculptures," Helena said doubtfully.

"What sculptures! No one would buy those things, not even for recycling."

Her daughter frowned like an illiterate person in front of a sign. "Not even for what?"

"Recycling, I mean turning what he says are sculptures into junk, since on their own they're junk, and from that junk, make something useful."

"Mamá!" Helena shouted.

Her mother sat thinking for a few seconds and then muttered to herself, "He must have stolen it. Where is he going to get money if he doesn't even know English? You and I know more, dear. The best teachers in the world couldn't teach that good-for-nothing."

"Ma, don't be so hard on him. Maybe he was nervous."

Her mother pulled a chair over to the bed and sat down slowly, like a member of a war tribunal about to interrogate the accused. "It could be. Was his voice trembling?"

"Yes."

"He must be using cocaine."

"No, I think it was trembling because he was really furious, because . . ."

"Nonsense," Dina interrupted her, "he must have been high on heroin. Did he ask for me?"

"Yes."

"What did he say?"

Helena tried to stop what she was about to say, but it was too late. Her brain had already sent the information to her lips. At that instant Helena realized that she no longer controlled her movements. They came automatically, having been transmitted thousandths of a second before. "That maybe you would find a husband in the United . . ."

The mother jumped out of her chair like a pilot reacting to news that his plane is about to crash. "Now that pig is playing matchmaker! Who told him I was looking for a husband?"

"I told him you weren't."

The mother raised her hands to her head. "And what did he say?"

Helena again regretted her actions, but her brain was accustomed to sending information unedited. "That a husband might help cure your neurosis."

"What a pity I wasn't here," she said, sitting down as if defeated.

"That's what I said."

Her mother sighed. "And what did he say?"

Her brain sent the information. "That it was late for you to be out and about."

"What business is it of his?"

Helena nodded. "That's just what I said to him."

Her mother looked grateful. "Well done, *hija,* I imagine that shut him up." Her daughter shook her head.

Dina came to life. "What do you mean no!"

"He told me to take a good look."

The professor hesitated, but chose to continue the interrogation. "Well," She paused. "At what?"

Her brain emitted the signal. "If you came home happy, it was a sign that you got laid . . ."

The noise of her mother's body jumping up cut her off. "I'm dying for him to call. That's all I needed. They go off to live in New York and look how arrogant they become! You will go through Miami, Helenita, I swear it. We'll move, if need be, we'll sell the house. It's too big for me, all alone. We'll move to an apartment until we find someone to buy it. That will give us a bit of money. We'll go, even without him. Even if I have to sell my soul to the devil."

Helena covered her mouth. "Mother!"

Dina made the sign of the cross. "Forgive me father, but I can't help myself. We're going."

Dina sat down again, trying to calm the anger that was raging through her. Memories of Helena's father came to mind, and she immediately saw similarities between what was happening to Helena with Elías and what had happened to her with her ex-husband. For her it was all an omen that Elías's situation would result in her daughter being the butt of the same joke. This was why she took on an occasional lover and often got too involved. In all men she saw the man who had left her dreaming of Miami. She stood up and, with the smile of someone in search of revenge, she swore, "We are going, but we will go via New York. We'll kill the pig and then go to Miami. I only hope God doesn't want us to run into that poor wretch of your father, for then there will be two murders."

Helena was frightened. "Mamá, you've never spoken like this!"

"This guy is not going to do to us what your father did. With men you never know, *m'ija*. Men are very good at making things up, and things that seem so real. That's what's so good about inventions: they seem real. You don't see the defects because you are in love. Just wait, you'll get over him."

"Elías is a good man. He loves me."

Dina sighed and pursed her lips, disappointed. "Life is as unfair as can be!"

Helena knew these expressions well. Dina would say things halfway so that Helena would ask what she was talking about and then she would air some complaint. Then she wouldn't feel so guilty, since, after all, she was just responding to a question.

Helena felt it was her obligation to ask her, even knowing she wouldn't like the answer. "What are you trying to tell me?"

"Nothing. You've said it all."

"I haven't said anything."

Her mother looked into her eyes. "Do you want me to repeat it?"

Helena's eyes tried to hide but there was nowhere to go, so she sat looking at her mother. "If you don't mind."

Dina spoke haltingly and with evenly measured syllables, like bread cut into slices. "Now-you-are-go-ing-to-lis-ten-to-that-ir-re-spon-si-ble-man-o-ver-your-own-mo-ther."

Sometimes Helena had the urge not to be a copy anymore. "That's what you said, not me."

"No, you did, because you're defending him so you can go. You're beginning to agree with him. You're defending him."

Her brain pounced. "We can't accuse him without any evidence. Are you convinced he stole or that his sculptures are going to make useful junk?"

The older copy sensed that the younger copy was about to rebel, and she decided to divert the conversation. "The word is 'recycle.'"

That was enough to bring the younger copy back in line. "It sounds nicer, but in the end it's the same. Besides, that's a difficult word."

The fragile possibility of rebellion was demolished like a dynamited building. The mother sat down on the bed and touched her daughter's hands. She picked up the right one and raised it to her chest, placing it as if taking an oath.

"What do you want more—to see Miami or to be with that good-for-nothing?"

Helena dropped her hand from her chest, not because she

disagreed, but in a signal that such protocols were not necessary to reaffirm the unconditional solidarity between the two. "Oh, Ma, what kind of question is that? Miami, of course." Her mother hugged her daughter, who lay her head on her mother's chest. Dina seemed to stare off into space, but she was traveling back in time.

"When you were just a baby, everything was so special," she said as she stroked her daughter's hair. "Your papá was still thinking about us back then. We made plans to live in Miami. At first he wasn't interested at all in traveling to the United States, and even less to Miami. But I dreamed that one day he would change his mind, and I spent my time clipping articles from newspapers and magazines about Miami. I would show him the photos of the Latin-American First Ladies on their November shopping trips and their June vacations, as well as the photos of the wives of our generals, colonels, and representatives. I was the one who showed him that many famous singers bought mansions in Miami. I also showed him videos of those highways, expressways, beaches, and those crowds of happy people in bathing suits. Later it was he who made sure he brought me everything that had to do with Miami. You were old enough then to understand some things, though not everything. When you would hear us talking about Miami, so focused on each other, you would walk in front of us to get our attention and you would say, 'Mommy, Poppy, and Helenita are going to fly in an airplane to Miami.'"

Dina wasn't telling a story anymore but reliving those moments with the same intensity with which they had occurred. Dina stroked Helena's hair, unaware that she was half-asleep, because the time machine had transported her back in time, and she was lost in the monologue of the little girl next to her who had now become a woman.

. . . They're going to buy me dresses and shoes and a crown so that I can be the queen of Miami. And Poppy is going to buy me a red car so I can drive down the streets (and you would open one of the magazines that was always on your nightstand, you knew them so well . . .) A red car like this one that messes up the girl's hair because there is no top. Why don't those cars have tops, Mommy? Doesn't it ever rain in Miami? And we'll go along the, along the, what did you say it was called, Pa? I know, don't tell me, now I remember: we'll go here, along the Palmetto Highway, passing all the other cars. My poppy driving over here, my mommy in the other seat so my poppy isn't alone, and me here, in the back, like my doll from Miami. Right, Mommy, you're going to buy me a doll from Miami? Blonde, blue-eyed, with long hair and high heels and skinny, so that no one calls her fat. Right, Poppy, you won't let anyone yell at my doll, will you? I'm going to tell my doll that when we go back to Tegucigalpa, I'll introduce her to my friends from school, and they'll want to be friends because I'm going to have a blonde doll from Miami, too. Poppy, it won't fall down, right? Why don't airplanes fall down, Ma? Mommy and Poppy and doll and Helenita, we'll all go to the beach, right, Ma? Like we saw on TV the other day, and you said, "There's nothing like Miami." Pa, you said you were leaving soon. Are you going to send for us? Why don't we go together, the three of us? Aren't there schools in Miami, Ma? In Miami there are only good things, pretty things, and if there are no schools, it should

be that way because schools aren't good or pretty. Mommy, why does Miami sound like Mommy? Mommy, Miami. Because it's pretty like you, Mommy, right, Pa? We'll bring the red car back here, and it will be the prettiest car in the world. And when I'm bigger, I'll drive it, right, Pa? Is it true that you don't know how to drive because you've never had one? Why aren't we rich or poor? What are we, Ma? I want to go to Miami now. I want the airplane to take us through the air to Miami so we can leave the world and buy the blonde doll and so Pa can learn to drive the red car and Ma can go swimming at the beach in a tiny bathing suit and . . .

Mother and daughter slept, nestled against each other like refugees of war.

The Statue of Fertility

Laura was getting things ready, for she was sure Elías would move in with her. She had lived long enough in large cities among artists in search of something. She had not spent so much time in San Francisco and Los Angeles for nothing, and now New York was part of her, too. She knew that sooner or later Elías would give in. It didn't matter why; it might be because he had nowhere to live, had to get his papers in order, whatever. She didn't care. Once she had him nearby, she would teach him to fall in love with her.

She was so sure of it that she even made a space in the apartment where Elías could work comfortably. She imagined the sculptor engrossed in his sweaty art, shirtless, his back glistening in the reflection of the sunlight, and she, stealing a few minutes of his time so he could have her with that natural taste of clay. She was intrigued by mummification. She wanted to be plastered from head to toe, left joyfully rigid in clay, and placed in a corner, like a full-body sculpture.

Elías had never even kissed her. It was she who brushed against his lips each time she said hello or goodbye. But it was more than just a feeling. She was sure that he liked her more than as a friend, and if he didn't dare kiss her back, it was because he had just arrived. She knew it was just a question of waiting until Elías could tear the map of his country from his skin and wrap himself up in the map of her body.

She did not usually build her hopes up, at least not without some reason, and Elías had given her that reason by never turning her down, except for the invitations to her apartment. She had other boyfriends whom she saw occasionally, but they disappeared after Elías arrived, maybe because in big cities there exists that ideal that those who have just arrived from small countries are the most suitable for an honest romance. Supposedly, they haven't been corrupted yet, still believe in love, and have not lost that air of innocence that the provinces instill. For her, Elías had all those virtues and two additional ones: He was an artist and he was very handsome. He was the right man to fulfill her dream of one day becoming a mother.

Everything went back to the way it was. The empty space was filled up again, the sculptor disappeared, the sunlight hid behind the curtain, she emerged from her thoughts, and, with that, the new mental design of her apartment evaporated as she slowly arose to get ready for work. She got out of bed and went to the shower, but not before turning on the music that filled her with life.

Darkness II

"I spoke to Helena yesterday."

"What did she say?"

"She's dying to come."

"When do you think you'll bring her here?"

"As soon as I can. I'm saving up."

"She may have to wait a year, then."

"No, never, she'll come soon."

"You don't make much money."

"I don't spend much, either."

"When she comes, you'll have more expenses. You'll have your own apartment."

"I know. Don't remind me. Are you throwing me out?"

"Not at all, you were a godsend. I was in debt. I'd rather have you pay me than pay for another more expensive place that's farther away."

"But when Helena . . . "

"Sure, I don't want you here forever, either. What if I find my other half?"

"You already have."

"No, I haven't, not yet."

"I'm not asking you, I'm telling you."

"Excuse me! I didn't know you knew more about my life than I did."

"Janeth . . . "

"Hmmmmmm . . . I like her, could be."

"She asked me about you."

"Why didn't you tell me before? That kind of information should be sent by fax."

"I haven't seen you much lately, even though we live in such a small place."

"That's New York."

"I'm beginning to see that."

"Talk to her about me. Tell her my good points, since she'll have time to discover my defects."

"That's a good one . . . Do you think it's true what they say, that Latinos are chauvinists?"

"Lies."

"Sometimes I think it could be true."

"Lies. It's a conspiracy against us."

"By whom?"

"The Latinas and the European and American men."

"Why?"

"So that the Europeans and Americans can take our women, and the Latinas can leave us without guilt."

"How smart!"

"Besides, they've maligned us. When European or American women see a Latino, the first thing they think of is machismo."

"Then you are taking the position that all Latinos are good?"

"I didn't say that. Of course, that's not true. There are Latinos who are very chauvinistic. But there are chauvinists in the rest of the world and the rest of the races, too, lots of them. But we are the only ones who have that label."

" I don't think I'm a male chauvinist."

"Why do you say that?"

"Yesterday, I spoke to Helena, and she was insisting on coming through Miami. A chauvinist would have told her what to do, and that would have been the end of it."

"Let her come any way she wants."

"Anyway she wants except through Miami."

"Let her. The important thing is that she gets here."

"That's precisely why I can't let her come through Miami, because I want her to get here."

"You're traumatized. Immigration is the same everywhere, especially for Latinos. They've declared war on us."

"No, in Miami they don't let anything slip by."

"They let you slip by, even when they were right. You only had a one-way ticket. It's the law."

"The very same thing would have happened if I had had a return ticket."

"They would be right, anyway. Your idea is to stay here, right?"

"Yes, but not illegally."

"So . . ."

"I'll ask for an extension."

"How are you going to pay a lawyer?"

"You sound like you're from immigration."

"A Latino's headache."

"She told me that if she didn't come through Miami, she wouldn't come at all."

"She'll come."

"She reminded me that she has no obligation to do as I say because we aren't married."

"What did you say to that?

"The logical thing. I told her she was right. I tried to make her happy."

"The logical thing? I would have hung up on her and never spoken to her again."

"I love her."

"Forget about her."

"It's different."

"You're naïve."

"Maybe, but I'll do everything I can to bring her here."

"Through Miami?"

"Never!"

"Then start looking for another girlfriend."

"Why?"

"Because you're weak. She won't listen to you."

"What should I do?"

"Be strong."

"How?"

"Tell her that she'll come the way you say or she should forget about you."

"But what if she thinks I'm serious and forgets about me?"

"You are serious."

"What if she decides to forget about me?"

"Beat her to it: forget her first."

"I can't."

"Don't be ridiculous. There's Laura, and a million other beautiful women just like her who are alone."

"Maybe you're right."

"I am."

"Telling her to come the way I say isn't chauvinistic, is it?"

"Who's paying for the ticket?"

"You know I am."

"Then it's not chauvinism; it's capitalism."

"It's clear, the dollar rules."

"You have a lot to learn, sculptor. Now, go to sleep."

"Are you sleepy?"

"A little."

"Do you think she'll listen to her mother over me?"

"What difference does it make? You told me her mother is dying to come to the United States, so . . ."

"Yes, but to Miami."

"Is she really hot?"

"Gorgeous, the old broad."

"Don't worry. Bring her over and then you can see about setting her up with one of those old neurotic retired guys that are all over Miami. Then you can get her off your back."

"You make it sound easy."

"It is easy."

"Then next time I should talk to her like a chauvinist?"

"No."

"Like a man?"

"No."

"Then?"

"Like the one who has the ticket."

"You've learned a lot."

"That's after ten years of living here."

"Do you think she'll do what I say and not come through Miami?"

"Uh-huh."

Rediscovering the Phone

In the old days, the only communication worry was if the postman—who would carry messages for long distances, conquering jungles, crossing rivers, exposing himself to other tribes, pursued by all types of wild animals and threatened by the effective poison of countless serpents—would reach his destination alive. There, the addressee, aware of the messenger's fatigue, would have him executed so he could rest eternally. Other means were used as the years went by, and so on, until the telephone came on the scene. And then came the fax.

A telephone message is to be listened to, and one has to more or less piece together what is said to be able to understand it. Naturally, there exists the possibility of recording the voice and listening over and over again, but that goes against good manners. So, only intelligence services around the world, which ignore the elementary rules of morality, commit that crime against humanity without burdening their consciences.

Although the telephone is no longer a novelty that surprises anyone, just like the computer and many other technological inventions, there are still people who, as if by ritual, huddle around a telephone, like our ancestors huddled around the fire in the dead of winter. Helena and her mother looked just like that: two women from ancient times who had discovered fire.

As soon as the sun rose, they quickly used their respective bathrooms, and then, with one pretext or another—such as reading, weaving, or trying to stay warm—they would huddle around the telephone, both pretending that that was not the magnetic object that was drawing them there.

There are many ways to wait for the telephone to ring when a call is expected, but the most frequent are: eagerly or fearfully. Eagerly, if a loved one says he will call that day; fearfully, if one has committed a crime and is sure that no one knows his telephone number. Dina and Helena were neither happy nor fearful. They were fierce soldiers of a tribe, waiting for the chief's war cry. Dina's tongue was an arrow eager to detect the enemy.

Since early that morning, the two women had hovered around the small varnished table that held the telephone that, depending on who was on the other end of the line, could spell either joy or disaster. The night announced its approach, and Dina asked Helena if she was hungry. She looked up from the magazine she was reading for a moment—fortunately, it was one of those magazines that does not require concentration—and, touching her stomach, said she was a few pounds overweight and that it wouldn't be a bad idea to fast for a day. Her mother approved of her dieting and supported her decision by fasting with her. The telephone did not ring anymore because her former friends from the upper class didn't call her anymore, and she had no friends from other classes. Therefore, when the telephone rang, there was no doubt that the call was from the only one, apart from themselves, who knew the number.

Helena felt that her relationship was breaking apart. The

technological silence in the house was the unequivocal end of her romantic dreams: her sculptor who would call her first thing in the morning, or not at all, because he worked nights. Her mother was right again: men were unstable, cold traitors. Dina swore never to respect them. Helena grew tired of the charade and threw the magazine at the wall.

"The good-for-nothing. He didn't call!"

Professor Dina was also growing tired of the drama. "I've told you time and time again."

"He must have met some Venezuelan girl."

Her mother looked pensive. "He'll call, even if it's just to insult us, he'll call. Besides, he has no one to call except for us, and they say that when people are in a foreign country, they feel the need to communicate with someone from their country. He may be drunk, but he is going to call. I don't know how much you love him, but I've always warned you that you should only love a man fifty percent. The other fifty percent should be reserved in the event he betrays you. That fifty, then, is for someone else, and from that fifty you should only give twenty-five percent to whomever comes next."

"Well," Helena said, downplaying herself, "it's not that I'm crazy about him, but like you yourself say, there's no such thing as love without self-interest, and there would be nothing better than taking our trip with him."

"We are going to go, anyway," Dina said authoritatively, "with or without him, we are going. Of course, it would be better to go with him because we wouldn't have to sell our house and all our things, especially because the Americans are deporting so many people . . . Can you imagine getting deported? What would become of us? He'll call."

Helena stood up and pulled her clothes tightly across her body. "I'm not really fat, Ma, am I?"

"No, no," her mother replied hastily, "you're beautiful, just lovely."

"Then I don't need to go on a diet," she said and smiled.

Her mother answered with a smile, and the two headed for the kitchen.

Getting Down to Business

Times were hard. Large-scale deportations of immigrants were being announced. Laws were changing with chilling speed. Latin Americans were the most pregnant target. There was talk of roundups and prison, and an occasional dead man on the Mexican border only increased the sense of uncertainty. Laura had given him a newspaper clipping that announced something called "Seminar on Immigration," which, in the face of the emergency that drove the hunt for immigrants, was to be a gathering of government representatives from Latin America, especially from those countries that were most affected. Elías worried about his status, but he also resisted these kinds of meetings. His experience with his country's apathetic leaders had caused him not to believe in anything or anyone in an official position. Nevertheless, more curious than eager to find a possible solution to his problem, he asked Mario to go with him.

* * *

When they entered the room, Elías's attention was drawn to a man near the door who was wearing glasses and had a scholarly beard and bright eyes that seemed to be deep in thought. The man reminded him of his uncle, the poet. The man noticed Elías's curious stare, smiled at him and signaled that he'd be coming over to say hello. Even though Elías noticed this, he was shy and hurried into the room to sit down. People were still arriving: there were people whose faces revealed genuine concern about the terrible situation that their fellow Latin Americans were in, and there were others who looked confused as to why they were there. A few representatives of Latin American governments seemed to be there only to take up space, but while their bodies were present, their hearts and minds were surely visiting places far removed from this situation, from which their diplomatic passports had delivered them.

The moderator called for everyone's attention. He was followed by the Argentine consul who, in a brief statement, made it clear that they were there to lend their support, but that his country was not affected by the problem. He said it in such a way that to Mario it seemed like Argentina was a faraway land that bordered Italy or France, a land that had nothing to do with Latin America. After that snub, Mario tried to leave, but Elías convinced him not to because he didn't want to stay alone with all those strangers who seemed so formal. Two other speakers got up and spoke and then, to Elías's surprise, the man with the scholarly beard walked to the front. The moderator introduced him: "And now please welcome Luis Moreno Guerra, consul of Ecuador in New York." Intrigued by the diplomat, they decided to stay. The ambassador used no microphone and stood there, facing the audience like an experienced political science professor. He got right to the point.

"I am going to begin with a question. U.S. anthropologist Stephen Shaybull said, 'What creature has successfully triumphed over the passage of time, achieved such extraordinary evolutionary development that it dominates earth, has transformed the environment, colonized most living beings, and can only progress and not regress?'"

The consul paused and saw the childish smiles from the audience shining up at him, like a professor who has just asked what two plus two equals. If this had been a class, all hands would have shot up at once, everyone wanting to be the one chosen by the professor to answer the question and impress the rest of the class. One Central American consul was smiling happily, as if to say that he and no one else was that creature referred to by Shaybull. For those who weren't as quick, that seemingly childish question revealed how superficial the answer would be.

The consul continued. "If this were an informal discussion, it would be interesting to open up the conversation to questions, but you already have the answer to those questions, more or less. What is the creature? The answer is obvious: bacteria."

The answer struck like lightning. Collective shame filled the room. Shame that none of those present had the privilege of considering themselves bacteria.

"A second question," the consul continued, facing the crowd who, because of the error they had made on the first question, were now hiding their hands so there would be no doubt they were not prepared to respond.

"What if the largest reptiles had not disappeared? What if dinosaurs had not become extinct? It seems their total disappearance left an ecological hole. If they had not disappeared, there would probably be no mammals, and the human being is a mammal."

Whispers rippled across the room. Someone said that the human being was a carnivore, another that his mother had never nursed him for fear of breast cancer.

"A third question: It is constantly pointed out that the

champions of the evolutionary race among mammals are the human being and the horse, and I would ask if that is so. The disappointing answer is no. If we go by the number of species and the degree of evolution reached among mammals, the highest marks go to the rat, the bat, and the antelope. The body that has evolved the most and needs no improvement from here on into the future is not the human being; it is the shark."

A wave of murmuring interrupted the speaker, especially among the Dominicans. They were staunch enemies of the shark because of the number of shipwrecks of undocumented people traveling from the island to the States, people who wound up as nothing but snacks for the selachians. Others, without even thinking about it, flatly denied the consul's statement that the rat and the bat were superior to them. No one said a thing about the antelope, for no one had a dictionary on hand.

"Why is this revelation so shocking?" the diplomat asked the audience, from which not a breath could be heard, a clear sign that the speaker's startling pronouncement had paralyzed them and that the speech would flow without any further interruptions. "How is it possible that this being, which is really so miniscule, from the zoological point of view, so incipient in the evolutionary process, is the only one that closes doors to others of its same species?

"This diminishes the arrogance of men, of the human being against other human beings. We may never be able to explain this variety of monkey. The number of our neurons and the way they function are so alarmingly limited that we are incapable of discovering our own origin. An accumulation of concurrent circumstances produced a chain of chemical reactions, causing the brain to evolve to the point of rationality.

"This variety of monkey was not the only one. We have

first cousins, another family of monkeys that also evolved to such a degree that they could use tools; but without explanation they disappeared. It is not a missing link; no, it was almost parallel evolution. How many previous processes were there? We don't know. We may know in the future. But what we do know is that in this variety of monkey, the process of rationality began. These monkeys could sit up, use tools, and their quality of life began to improve. However, according to anthropologists, adaptation with improvements that is not to some degree evolution, began thousands of years ago in Africa in what is today the Republic of Mozambique."

Mario elbowed Elías. "Wow! This guy sure knows how to get down to business!"

Elías motioned for him to be quiet. "Then they moved on to Europe, then Asia, and it seems that in Asia the process of rationality, not evolution, culminated, because ever since human beings were armed with rationality, they became the most savage and repugnant beasts when at war, and war was the daily bread. So the human being was not king and we are not in an evolutionary process of improvement, unless it was an effort of individual or collective consciousness that given these serious limitations, we assumed the collective compromise of overcoming our deficiencies and misery.

"When this colonization of the only rational species had covered Europe and Asia and spread to what is now America, geographers explain that in the era of the deep freeze the sea level was much lower and this allowed one to cross what is now the Bering Strait on tiptoe; that was not a geographical obstacle to migrations.

"The first Mongols arrived and began to settle on virgin lands, and everyone settled in the spot according to the horizon with which they identified. It is true that when the subsequent waves of Mongols came to America, appearing in Alaska, they found no uniformed officer asking for passports, visas, absentee taxes, or proof of vaccines, nor were there the repugnant customs types searching through bags, inflicting collective humiliation.

"Back then, they came in without any of these traps. Those were the days when human beings were able to make use of their inherent right to mobility and relocation, or in the words of Gabriel García Márquez, 'when people were happy and undocumented.'

"Then this so-called evolution or progress was eliminated, and the right to mobility and relocation began to shrink, to become more limited or was annihilated completely, and the fief appeared and created the border. Why? In order to define the precise limits of the feudal lord's domain and also so he would know where he could expand at the expense of others. The feudal lord's justification was that his authority came directly from God, and so the serfs could not revolt against the feudal lord because that would be challenging God himself. If God had given them the authority, no one said where or how, but that is what was said. There was no way to revolt; one had to resign oneself to being a slave.

"These two characteristics of the fief passed on to the state. The state was a very new judicial entity, an intellect, a creation of human beings. While it was very new, it was already very old, obsolete, out-dated and unable to withstand new changes. The state inherited the feudal concept of divine authority in order to be sovereign, and the border became the limit. In that way, the planet earth was divided into corrals called states, and inside, human beings acted like domesticated animals, 'entrance prohibited, exit prohibited.' The inherent, inalienable right of mobility and relocation was gone, and modern states replaced the feudal lord, because in the fief it was only comfortable and safe in the castle, at the expense of the serfs, and each feudal lord had ten thousand slaves.

"The world hasn't changed, for the so-called feudal states and feudal lords are now called super powers, and the serfs are the third-world countries. Now if someone wants the benefits of work, education, health, recreation, the ability to save, they go to the feudal lord's castle, which today is called an industrialized power, because he who does not enter the castle has nothing, like the serf who did not even own his land or his animals or his wife or his children or even himself. That is the Third World. If they don't want the 'serfs' to start jumping over the castle walls, well, then something must be done; some of that wealth must be distributed to them so that they can have food and satisfy their basic needs. Migrations are spontaneous, natural, legitimate movements that do not stop because of laws, rules, prohibitions, or sanctions. Walls and ramparts are of no use.

"If migrations are understood as legitimate individual and collective rights, the only problem this reveals is the xenophobic attitude of turning away people who are in search of a better life. Who is this immigrant? The immigrant is an exceptional being; he is courageous, risking his life for an unknown destiny, motivated by an internal, unsuspecting force: the desire to improve his condition, for himself and his family. That is why the immigrant does the jobs that the native won't, and here is the myth: that the immigrant comes and takes jobs away from others. This is a lie. Here it is more comfortable to receive money for not doing anything than for doing a job you don't like.

"All rich societies have both employed and unemployed people because it is a way of controlling the manpower. If there is full employment, there is also a danger, because the price of manpower rises along with the price of products, and it becomes cheaper to pay people not to do anything. From the moral point of view, it is immoral, but that is the reality. The myth that the immigrant takes jobs away is beginning to fade. The immigrant actually generates more jobs than he takes, and the jobs he takes are those the native doesn't want to do, anyway. What would happen to rich countries if all the immigrants left? They would collapse. Who would do those thankless jobs at the wages paid to the immigrants? No one.

"There is another myth: that the immigrant ruins society. The poor immigrant is probably unaware that here, throwing a paper on the street is frowned upon. But from the point of view of crimes committed, immigrants are among the lowest perpetrators. They are the ones who contribute, pay taxes, and receive the least, and so there is no justification for the anti-immigrant attitude. It is unfair, untrue, and ungrateful, because all human beings at one point in time are, were, or will be immigrants.

"I could elaborate, but because of our limited time I would like to conclude with one thought: It is said that eggs and human beings are alike because they were not made by walking on them. Thank you."

There was a burst of applause, some sincere and some simply out of inertia, but the result, which does not distinguish between real and fictitious applause, was unanimous approval of the consul's speech.

Mario was happy. "Thanks for asking me to come. It was

worth coming just to hear him."

Elías smiled. "I didn't expect this, either."

"Should we go?"

"Yeah, but let me say hello to him first."

They waited a few minutes until the reception had official-ly begun. Elías made his way through the crowd of people gathered around the consul in order to congratulate him. The diplomat smiled and accepted the compliment humbly, and this made Elías feel like calling him Luis, without academic or diplomatic title, just Luis, plain and simple. He didn't dare, however, out of shyness and because of the circumstances. But the consul's eyes told him that they were of the same mind, that they were among those that can't live without thinking and contributing their part in search of a better world.

They returned home, satisfied. Mario, given to philoso-phizing, saw in the consul the diplomat that he would have been had he not decided to emigrate in search of different things. The influence of his family and his intellect would have had him in a position similar to and compatible with the con-sul's. Elías denied that there were more opportunists in his country than servants of the people, and he emphasized the ignorance of most of the government officials in his country, both inside and outside of Honduras.

Content, Elías said to Mario, "Okay, I didn't get residency, but that speech made it worthwhile."

"Yeah." Mario smiled. "Luis Moreno Guerra. Sounds like an emperor. With the middle name of a slave, and a last name that doesn't exactly sound like a pacifist. Life shows us once again that appearances can be deceiving. He's brilliant. It was worth going, even though you already have your residency, and even citizenship, if you want it."

"Why do you say that?"

"Laura, marry her. Don't be a fool."

"No, I don't need to. Honduras served the United States more than any other country in the war against the Communists in Central America. This country has a moral obligation not to make it hard for us."

"You animal, you should be ashamed of yourself, using the death and torture of your fellow countrymen to try and settle here."

"The end justifies the means."

"Not always, not with all the blood spilled in Central America. It would be more honorable, even Machiavelli would congratulate you, if you married Laura."

Window to Hell

Mario leaned against the bar, the place reserved for singles. The bartender was the companion of all who were alone. A bartender who is reluctant to talk with the customers is no bartender, and will, therefore, be forever unemployed. And the single person never sits at a table because this just magnifies his solitude. Good restaurants do not have tables for one. They always leave two chairs at a table; then, if someone is eating alone, the empty chair leaves open the possibility that someone could be there, eating with him. Without the empty chair there, the solitude produced by the other end of the table is greater; it's like the window to one of those black holes in space, which for many is hell.

Though Mario had been single for a long time, he was not fond of hell. He preferred the bar that brought all the single people together, so they weren't single anymore. At the bar, it's easy to talk to whomever is next to you, while it's not wise to talk from one table to the next. At the bar, Mario could talk to the bartender and at the same time keep an eye on Janeth, who, knowing she was being watched, behaved coquettishly as she walked around and served tables. From time to time Janeth walked by Mario to tell him something, which was nothing more than the small steps that lead to romance.

Elías had already told the bartender that whatever Mario ordered was to go on his tab. That was just a polite formality, since the bartender wasn't going to charge anybody anything but would put it all on the house. Janeth looked happier than usual. When she had the chance, she would chat up Elías, trying to find out more about Mario, but no one knew much about him, just that he was a photographer who had lived in New York for more than a decade, was single, and didn't like to talk about his past or his future and only a little about the present. He was also very cautious when it came to matters of love. He calculated everything with the coldness of someone who had a tragic past. He had never really looked for a woman with whom he could have a serious relationship, just one who would be a companion for a time, with whom he could make love, while both maintained their own places, never violating the barriers of their own individuality.

What Mario did not suspect was that Laura and Janeth were conspiring to get both him and Elías. Neither Laura nor Janeth gave the idea of a fleeting romance a thought. They were sure that destiny had put those two men there for them, and the fact that their feelings had in some way been reciprocated nourished their convictions.

On her lunch break, Janeth asked Mario to join her. He accepted gladly, and at that time they agreed that after work they would go to a club with Laura and Elías.

The Myth Come Undone

Even when he was half-drunk, Elías kept his distance. Mario, on the other hand, knew why he was there. He was holding Janeth's hand, hugging her at times and giving her an occasional kiss on the cheek, and when they were dancing and their bodies pressed together, it almost looked like they were making love.

Mario returned to the table with his arm around Janeth's waist. When there was enough light, he winked at Elías and made a motion urging him to make his move. Elías missed this, and Mario said, "Poor Laura, don't you see that this man is in love with a crazy woman in Tegucigalpa. Crazy in the truest sense of the word, both mother and daughter."

Laura and Janeth laughed.

"Tell us," Laura said, taking Elias's hand.

Elías was grateful for the darkness of the disco. He was filled with shame and an overwhelming desire to end the party. "Don't listen to him. He's been drinking. He says all sorts of foolish things when he has a few too many."

"Too many drinks," Mario repeated. "Wake up, sculptor, those old broads are trying to cheat you. Don't you see how ridiculous their obsession with Miami is? They saw airline tickets written all over your face."

The women laughed again.

"Tell us," Laura insisted, "is it true?"

A song came on to save him, like a rope thrown to someone sinking in quicksand.

Elías took hold. "Let's dance instead," he said to Laura,
taking her by the hand and leading her to the dance floor.
Laura wrapped her arms around his neck, and with every
intention in the world, but being casual about it, she rested her
lips on his neck. A chill sped through Elías from head to toe.
He wasn't sure if it would have been better just to have put up
with Mario's jokes rather or dance his way out. Elías liked her,
which was the only reason he didn't give in. He could have
slept with any other woman and not felt unfaithful to Helena,
but not with Laura. Going further would mean going all the
way.

Laura gradually moved her head until their lips brushed
against each other. She opened her mouth and began slowly to
bite his closed lips. The map of his country began to vanish
from his skin, rolling up like a blueprint an architect decides
not to use again. He responded to the kiss with his eyes closed,
hoping to lessen the sin. The kiss carried them away, and they
felt like two pairs of lips dancing alone, bodyless, suspended in
the air.

Elías overheard a voice say "Should we imitate them?" He
recognized the voice, and while the prolonged kiss continued,
he half-opened his eyes to see Mario and Janeth dancing nearby, imitating them. Elías couldn't help laughing, and he pointed the couple out to Laura, who laughed, too. They kept laughing for no reason at all, since it didn't make sense that they
would be laughing at something as common as a couple kiss-
ing on the dance floor of a disco. They continued laughing
until they got back to the table. Janeth and Mario followed
them, and they, too, were laughing for no apparent reason.

"The myth has been broken," Mario said.

"Yeah, yeah," Elías said, "you're drunk."

Mario laughed. "Today you've taken a good second step, congratulations."

"What was the first?" Laura asked.

"He was supposed to call those old broads in Tegucigalpa three days ago, and he hasn't called them, even though he's dying to."

"Is that true?" Janeth said, smiling maliciously.

Elías adopted a more serious tone. "Yes, it's true. I have a girlfriend, and I love her. She's going to come live with me. What's so mysterious about that? And now I'm leaving. For me, the party is over." As he said this, he stood up.

Laura hugged him. "Don't be silly."

"Yeah, don't be a killjoy," Mario seconded.

Janeth chimed in, "Calm down, calm down, Elías."

He sat down again. "All right, but let's change the subject. I don't want to talk about this anymore."

"Okay," Mario agreed.

The men now turned their attention to their respective dates.

"When is she coming?" Laura asked.

"I don't know exactly," he replied, feeling uncomfortable.

"Why didn't you tell me?"

"There was no reason to tell you."

"You responded to my flirtations."

He ran his hand through her hair. "Because I like you. I like you a lot. You have to understand that this is hard for me. We work together, and I wouldn't want to hurt you."

"You won't hurt me. When she comes, I'll know how to understand."

"And what about me? Don't you think it would hurt me to be with you and then suddenly have to leave you?"

"You have to live in the present," she said, stroking his chin. "She's far away right now, and we are here."

"You're right; theoretically, it's easy. The problem is that in reality it's complicated."

"I promise you that I'll accept whatever you decide, but in the meantime we can be good friends."

He gave her a quick, gentle kiss. "Not even you believe that."

"I'm serious. It won't be easy, but I'll do it."

"When is the wedding?" Mario interrupted. "Janeth and I agree to be the maid of honor and best man."

"Yeah, sure," Janeth said, smiling.

"We're not in a hurry." Laura laughed.

"I think we should leave now," Elías proposed. "Almost everyone's gone, and we don't want to wait for them to throw us out."

"Where are you going to sleep?" Mario asked.

Elías smiled. "Where I pay rent."

"We'll drop you off," Janeth said, car keys in hand, "and then we'll continue the party."

"Really?" Elías said, surprised.

"Are you jealous?" Laura asked.

A Festering Wound

It had only been two weeks since that night in the disco, and Mario was already waking up every morning in Janeth's apartment. He opened his eyes and, deep in thought, stared at the ceiling. She was sleeping, her back turned toward him. He turned on his side to face her. She was so close and doubly vulnerable, both naked and asleep. He looked at her back and ran his finger gently across the back of her neck, then down her back to her buttocks, as if it were a pencil scribbling on her skin. He touched one buttock and then the other. He caressed it with the palm of his hand, and then moved down in search of her thighs. Still asleep, she half-opened her legs. He let his hand rest on her most intimate part and left it there as he kissed her gently, careful not to wake her up.

He had not had a girlfriend for a long time. He hadn't wanted one. All of his relationships were ephemeral. Some years before, he had almost married, but the engagement was broken off for a ridiculous reason.

Mario had been involved in politics in his country since his youth, when he had been a student activist in a leftist organization. The avalanche caused by the crumbling of the Soviet Union had consequences around the world, and his country was no exception. Mario accepted the triumph of the right-wing opponent courageously and with dignity, unlike many who denied having been on the left, who were ashamed and tried to erase their activist past among the Communist ranks the way one might try to deny being infected with the black plague. Mario decided not to stay in his country because he was disgusted by the sight of former Communists, who not long ago had condemned government corruption and had given speeches in support of the working class. Now these former activists were fighting with each other over a ministry post, dropping to their knees in the hopes of gaining some spot in the government, and joining as quickly as possible the long line of unscrupulous public servants who had nibbled away at public funds, who shamelessly sold the country to the highest bidder. Many of those who previously had called themselves comrades, who had traveled for free to Communist countries like leaders of a new society, now revealed their true faces, casting off their masks, exposing themselves as parasites eager to wallow in the dregs of power.

Even though he had left his country and made his home in New York City, it was impossible to detach himself, as he had originally intended, from the political situation in Latin America. He had been an activist of conviction, the kind who never abandons his ideals. Although conditions were nothing like they were during the Cold War, the same problems still existed in Latin America. Those countries were not affected in the slightest by the end of the Cold War. The cease-fire did not stop the killing, crime increased because of the economic crises, and government intensified its level of corruption. In short, nothing had changed. It was that ideological fervor that made him end his relationship with his girlfriend, a relationship that had had great promise; he had fallen in love. Political shortsightedness had disarmed him once again. When the United States invaded Panama, he cried out of sadness and helplessness for not being able to do anything about it. He felt more like a traitor than ever, living in the country that specialized in invading others, in dictating the rules to be followed in all aspects of life. On television, he watched those scenes of Marines firing amidst clouds of smoke in Panama City and he knew he was a coward. The only thing he could do with his indignation was take revenge upon the person least responsible, his girlfriend. She was from the United States, but she was completely ignorant about not only her country's politics beyond its own borders but about politics in general. She did not know anything nor did she care; politicians and politics had never interested her. If she were asked her opinion about some political matter or some politician, she probably would not have been able to respond, or worse, she would say what she had once said while she and Mario were watching television. She had asked him to change the channel because it was too boring to watch those fat old men who were just looking for someone else to go to war with.

Mario tried to get over the invasion of Panama and his relationship. He was able to do so for a few days, but there was that unhealed and festering wound. He remembered the history of Latin America and out would ooze the pus of resentment that sometimes spilled onto Spain and other times the United States. He would stroke his girlfriend's blonde hair, and, all of a sudden, the wound would appear, telling him that between him and a girl with blonde hair and white skin there could be no friendship, much less romance. The wound would close up again, but the slightest incident would cause it to fester and reopen.

Mario hugged Janeth and clung to her body as if by doing so he would forever bury his thoughts about the stupid breakup with his ex-girlfriend. Several years had passed, and as he hugged that woman, breathing in her scent, and softly pressing his flaccid member against her white buttocks, something told him that he was ready to start over, without giving that wound a chance to spew out the pus of absurdity.

Only Shadows

"Living in countries like ours is a disgrace." Dina's voice was heard over the sound of objects being moved and then falling, as she rummaged for a flashlight. "I'm sure the lights never go out in Miami. Blackouts only happen in miserable countries like thi . . . "

"All right, Ma," Helena interrupted her, "you don't have to be so critical. It's our country, after all."

"Who knows," she said as objects continued falling to the ground. "I think some people are born in the wrong place by accident. We don't have Indian or black features, and that must mean that we should have been born in Europe. There are Europeans who should have been born in the jungle, too, and wear loincloths like the Africans do."

"Ma, you'd better sit down; you're going to hurt yourself."

"I found it! Now all I need is for the batteries to be dead."

"Ah, Ma, get that light out of my face."

"You can't talk to someone without seeing their face. The words and the face often say different things."

Helena's face was trapped in a circle of light. "It's rude to shine a light into someone's face. Besides, I can't see your face, either."

"You don't need to see my face because I'm your mother.

I speak to you with my heart, not my voice or my face."

"But I'm your daughter," she said, closing her eyes to the light.

"Precisely. Children are those who lie most to their parents. Anyway, it's not my fault you have no flashlight to shine on me. If you had found it first, democracy would give you the right to shine it on me."

"But I never lie to you," Helena said, leaning her head back against the sofa.

Her mother remained standing, shining the light into her face.

"I know. I'm talking about children in general. Not you, Helenita. You're an exception. That's why I can listen to you without seeing your face." Her mother held the flashlight on her chest and turned the light on herself, illuminating her face. "Say something. See how I trust you."

"I don't have anything to say. Take that light off your face; you're scaring me."

"Am I that ugly, Helenita?" She sent the light back over to her daughter's face.

"No, you're beautiful, but that light would make anyone look frightful, even Miss Venezuela. Take that inhuman light off me!"

"If you want to succeed in this world and in big cities like Miami, you should drop that silly idea of humanism. That is something that belongs to Third World countries, and we will soon belong to civilization."

"That's terrifying."

"What's terrifying?"

"What you just said."

Her mother sat down on the sofa next to her, removed the light from her face and sent it up to the ceiling. "It's true. That's the modern world."

"I don't know what to think."

"It's better not to think at all," she said, illuminating her face once again.

"Take that light off me."

"No, we are talking about important things. I have to study your face to see if you are capable of leaving the Third World behind."

"It must be the same everywhere."

"What must be the same?"

"There must be some people who are more human and others who are less human."

"Nonsense, *hija*. Humanism is the Communism of the future. You'll see. They'll pursue them, put them in jail, or they will just disappear."

"Let's hope you aren't being prophetic."

"Yes, let's hope so," her mother said, just as the electricity came back on.

From the streets there were cries of joy celebrating the return of the light. Dina turned off the flashlight.

Helena sighed. "Do you think Elías has forgotten all about me?" she said.

"He'll call, he loves you, he'll call. When he runs out of money. That's how men are. He may be dying to call you. You'll see, he'll call soon."

"Maybe he's already met an American girl."

"No, dear. You have to have money, not just a pretty face, to have a woman there."

Helena cheered up. "At last you admit that he's handsome!"

"I didn't say that because of him," her mother said, puckering her lips together like a fish and shifting them to one side.

"I think he's very good-looking."

"All young people are good-looking."

"Even him?"

"What can I say."

Helena laid her hand on her mother's leg. "Thank you, Ma."

"What for, if the good-for-nothing isn't going to call you again, anyway?"

"I'm saying it because of me, not him. It means I have good taste."

"Of course you do, but my decision is still the same. You are not going unless you go through Miami."

"Of course, that won't change. We'll have to go to *Nueva York* first, though, and from there we'll go to Miami."

"It's New York," her mother corrected her. "I'm not sure. You only get one chance in life. Suppose something happens?"

Her daughter looked frightened. "Like . . . ?"

"We get deported. It's more and more difficult for Hispanic immigrants . . . especially for illegals. In California they actually hunt them."

"How do you know? You've never lived there."

"*Ay, m'ijita,* I know more about the United States than even the Library of Congress in Washington."

"Oh, Ma, you make me so proud. There's no one like you."

"You, too, darling, you've learned how to use the *tú* so wonderfully."

"Like Venezuelan women, Ma?"

"Nonsense, a thousand times better!"

Helena got up and stood in front of the mirror. "Ah, you're just saying that because I'm your daughter."

"No, I'm not the only one who says so. Other people do, too. My friends who we visited last week told me so. And the people at the store said so, too."

"Now I understand Elías. It comes naturally; all of a sudden, you don't even realize what you are saying."

"Of course, in other countries you have to learn to speak other languages and in other ways."

"My English is not bad. *What did you say?*" Helenita said, practicing her English.

"*Is perfect, honey,*" her mother replied in broken English. "*Your English is wonderful. You're ready for Miami.*"

"Yeah, but it's been three months, and he hasn't called or written."

Her mother sat thinking for a few seconds. "The way he spells, it's better he doesn't write. You'll have to call him. If it doesn't work out, we'll use my savings and the money from the sale of the house to go. We'll make a new life. Who knows, maybe Elías is right. Maybe I'll get married in Miami."

"Ma, I don't know."

"What don't you know?"

"I don't know if I'm still in love with Elías. So much time has gone by."

"It hasn't been that long."

"But I'm not sure."

"When you see him, you'll be sure. You'll see that you love him just like you did before, or maybe even more."

"I suppose it's possible. But what if I don't? I wouldn't want to lead him on." Helena sat back down next to her mother.

"I know, *hija,*" she said, stroking her hair. "I know you have a good heart. We women are wonderful, and for nothing really, because the men just take up with another or leave us altogether."

"Yes, but not all men. There have to be some good ones, Ma."

"Yes, the Europeans and the Americans. These Latinos are a bunch of *machos.*"

"And you're sure that Europeans and Americans are good? On TV I saw that an American guy killed his wife and ate her piece by piece. He kept her in the refrigerator."

"He did that out of love, out of great passion."

"Ma, how can you say that! He's a murderer. I also saw that a Spaniard hit his wife out of jealousy."

"Well . . . there are exceptions, naturally."

"What will the men be like in Miami?"

Her mother's face lit up. "*Ay, hijita,* that I don't know, but I picture them wearing dark glasses, open shirts showing their chest hair, and bright-colored shorts . . . . No, *hija,* a man dressed like that has to be different."

Helena also began to dream. "I imagine them the way they are in the movies."

"You have to call Elías. We have to move to Miami. I was born to be a First Lady, and if I had been, I would only vacation in Miami. I was born to be a fine *señora,* but sadly I picked the wrong man. See? Mistakes are expensive. That irresponsible father of yours . . . "

"Better late than never. We'll go. I promise to send for you soon, in no more than two months."

"That will be the happiest day of my life!"

"Should I call?" she asked, looking over at the telephone.

"Well, we won't be paying for the call anyway, so yes. Let's call."

Outside there were cries of indignation as the lights went out again. Helena, with an unaccustomed reflex, grabbed the flashlight.

Elías's Debut

The exhibition was ready. Elías was walking about the gallery as one does just minutes before an opening, smoking one cigarette after another and looking over his sculptures from various angles. The one he had made from the handlebars seemed to stand out. It had no special shape, but it grabbed your attention for the intensity of the blue and red with which he had painted it.

"Don't be so nervous," the owner of the gallery said. "Have faith. People will come. Painters who are now millionaires and sculptors who are now doing well have all passed through this gallery. This place is small but prestigious. I'm exhibiting your work because you're a friend of Laura's. She's a charming woman; it's not easy to convince me when the artist is a complete unknown, like you. But I support love, just like years ago they supported me in Cali . . . She's crazy about you."

"I'm com-plete-ly known. I am very well known in my country."

"That's wonderful, but that was there. You don't gain anything here by being known there. The important thing in New York is to be known in New York."

Elías lowered his voice. "But it helps that in one's country, the people . . . "

"There's no such thing. It doesn't matter. Not even awards in foreign countries are taken into account here, except, of course, those in some European countries. Who knows you in your country?"

"Well, people do. My exhibitions have been reviewed, and I've been written up in the social pages of all the newspapers there, so . . ."

The gallery owner turned on the light and lowered it a bit, looking for the perfect shading.

"Look, I'm not interested in your stories. I know Latin America well. They're all the same: a bunch of drunks know you."

"My work has been shown in several countries," Elías tried to explain, but without conviction.

The woman left a dim light illuminating one of the sculptures.

"Let's say that's true. What good is that here? That means nothing here. Walk one block and you'll meet artists who are well known in their countries, and here they are nobodies, because they haven't succeeded here."

A male voice was heard offering an effusive greeting that filled the small gallery. "Hello, everyone, I'm interested in buying that sculpture of the handlebars." After announcing this he roared with laughter.

The woman looked at Mario and shook her head from side to side. "This is no time for jokes. Look how nervous he is, and you're making it worse. I'll be right back. I have to see if the wine and cheese are ready."

The woman disappeared through a rear door. Mario put a

new roll of film in his camera and began to focus on various objects, testing the lens.

Elías seized their moment alone and said, "Three months and she still hasn't called."

Mario focused the camera on Elías's face. "Come on, cut it out; she's going to call. Her mother is probably telling her to wait for you to call so they'll make you give in."

"I'm not going to call her. I've made up my mind," Elías said, staring into the camera's eye.

"That's the best thing you can do. If I were you and had Laura, I would have forgotten about her already. That woman has it all, man. Are you blind? You shouldn't even have to think twice about marrying her."

"I could say the same about Janeth."

"At least, I'm thinking about it," he said as he focused on one of the sculptures.

"Are you serious?"

"Of course, I'm serious." Mario dropped his camera, letting it dangle from his neck. He looked at Elías. "The invasion of Panama wasn't her fault."

Elías frowned, trying to figure out what he thought was a joke. "I don't get it."

"It's not a joke. She's not responsible for the Sandinistas losing power in Nicaragua, either, or the assassination of Salvador Allende, or the war in El Salvador that left so many dead, or the 30,000 who disappeared in Argentina, or the fact that Honduras has been converted into a huge military base, or for Costa Rica becoming an accomplice of the United States or for the ongoing mistreatment of the Guatemalans . . . "

"That's politics. It has nothing to do with love."

"Of course, it does," Mario said, sitting down on a bench. "How many times does a man like a girl, but because she's from a country we regard as an enemy or one that has historical debts with us, we can't see her as she is but rather only as the enemy?"

"I've never looked at anyone from that perspective before. To me, people are people."

"Sure, like the immigration officer told you, you shouldn't be so cynical, treating Morazán and Hitler the same way. You have that void that you call apolitical, which is really nothing more than cowardice, fear of facing reality."

Elías searched in the inside and outside pockets of his jacket for his cigarettes. "Maybe you're right, but people are people, and governments are governments. People can love, governments can't. Governments are there to hate. Governments don't even love their own countrymen. Of course, this is more true of some than others. Our own Latin governments are known for and excel in hating their own people, or am I wrong? If they didn't hate their countrymen, they wouldn't steal so much. They wouldn't sell the country to foreigners for ridiculous prices; they wouldn't order armies to massacre the people when they are only demanding their rights. What do you say to that? People love and governments hate. A simple citizen has no voice or vote in a government that is going to commit an atrocity inside or outside of its country. A poor citizen is no more than that, a poor citizen."

Mario burst out laughing. "Congratulations. I see that you don't have a void, but that you are hypocritical. You just gave a political speech, Mr. Apolitical."

"Do you have a cigarette?"

Mario shook his head.

"Getting back to what we were talking about, it's true, Laura is beautiful, maybe even more beautiful than Helena. But it's not the same. I like Laura and I love Helena."

"Don't get all sentimental. Today is your New York debut. You're going to be at odds with your work. The irreverent author of the sculpture of the bicycle handlebars is a romantic. Make up your mind. Don't call her ever again, or call her and tell her to come any way she wants. After all, what do you have to lose?"

"I'll lose her. She can come any way she wants, except through Miami."

Mario got up and looked out onto the street. "You are a talented artist, Elías, except for your masterpiece, 'The Bicycle Handlebars.' You can't continue to live as you are, traumatized by an insignificant thing like what happened in Miami."

"Insignificant? If you had gone through what I did, you wouldn't say that. My work, by the way, is not called 'The Bicycle Handlebars.' It's called 'Before the Future,' or in Spanish, 'Antes del Futuro.' Nice title, don't you think?"

"I still think there's time to not show that thing; it's in such bad taste," he said, looking over at the sculpture. "Don't forget that in New York, recycling is the law."

"I wouldn't not show it for anything in the world," he responded, continuing to search for the cigarettes he knew he didn't have. "I've seen many exhibitions, and I'm telling you that there are horrible things, garbage. At least I gave form to this work of art, and I painted it."

"All right, all right . . . just don't call it a work of art in front of me."

"Okay, whatever you want, but don't ask me not to show it. I'm even starting to like it. Honestly."

Mario let out an infectious laugh. "I hope you're joking."

Elías laughed, too. "Well, yes. Don't be so suspicious of art, either."

"There's a bar just around the corner. While there's still time, let's go get some cigarettes, and you can have a drink to steady your nerves and chase away bad memories."

Recycling Is the Law

"Where could they have gone?" Laura asked.

"I don't know," the gallery owner replied. "They were here when I left. Fortunately, nobody was interested in stealing the sculptures."

"Maybe they went to a bar," Janeth speculated. "That's what artists do."

The small gallery continued to fill up with people. Laura spoke with each visitor, as if she were the creator of the sculptures. The people formed small circles of three or four and spoke about topics unrelated to art. Wine was now in the hands of many people. Some would stop for a few seconds in front of a sculpture and then continue on to the next, with their expressions unchanged, revealing neither approval nor disapproval. Laura looked on, bothered by those eccentricities typical of art viewers. Janeth was anxious, too, waiting for the sculptor to return, not because of him but because of whom he was with, Mario.

When they returned, Elías felt the nerves again that had vanished at the bar. He felt an inexplicable shame for being the artist for whom all those people had gathered. He didn't want anyone to know who he was. He thought about how he should behave, for he was sure Laura would introduce him around. After all, she was the one responsible for the exhibition. Finding himself among all those people grouped around his work made him want to escape.

From time to time, someone would approach him to congratulate him, and he couldn't believe it. He managed a smile and acted happy, but inside he wondered, how clean the world would be if people were congratulated for picking up junk.

In Praise of Junk

A gay couple entered the gallery. They were making a lot of noise and laughing about something, and they moved through the crowd with the magic of an "excuse me." They were followed by two women who were holding hands; they were dressed in black, with large, black shoes. One of the men who had made his way through the crowd slowly walked up to the sculpture of the bicycle handlebar. His clothes gave him away as being gay; his voice and mannerisms confirmed it.

"What's this!" he exclaimed, placing his two index fingers on each side of his forehead as if he had horns. "I'm a bull, muuuu . . . " and he pretended he was going to charge his friend. They both laughed, and he said, "What are you doing? You have to say *olé* . . . ."

Laura, who was not far away, said, "Just what we needed. I thought this was going to be a civilized event."

The gay man replied, "What's happening? *Yo entiende un poquito de español,*" and he made the same gesture with the horns, acting like he was going to attack Laura.

She smiled, and replied in English, "Are you crazy?"

He took on a more serious demeanor, and in broken Spanish spoke to Laura. "*¿Qué ser esa escultura?*"

"I don't know what it is. Do you speak Spanish?" Laura asked.

"A little."

"Okay, then go ask the artist."

"Where is he?"

Laura pointed toward Elías with her eyes. "He's right over there."

Elías walked over to them. "Did you call me?"

"Yes, ¿qué ser esto?" the gay man asked, almost touching the sculpture.

"The name is right here," was all he replied, conveying the little interest he had in talking.

The gay man leaned over to read, then burst out laughing. 'Before the Future.' Pero ¿qué ser esto?"

"It's abstract," Elías said, annoyed.

The gay man winked at him. "Tell me the truth."

"Modern art."

The girls in black were still holding hands as they followed the conversation about the sculpture. The gay men continued laughing.

"Change the title. Call it 'Modern Art' and I'll buy it."

The conversation came to an end when Laura's eyes invited the others to look toward the door, where a man had appeared dressed in a suit with white shoes and a hat, seeming to step right out of a movie. Two men in black suits, who looked like bodyguards, trailed behind him. The man in the white hat straightened his dark glasses and appeared to be interested in looking at the sculptures. He moved from one to another, and while all continued their conversations, almost everyone seemed to sneak a glance at that man with the white hat. He stopped in front of the sculpture of the handlebars. He concentrated, as if he was studying every detail, took off his glasses, cleaned them, and put them back on.

Excited, he exclaimed, "Oh, God, oh my God, I can't believe it! This is great, it's incredible, it's fantastic! Oh, God." The bodyguards had not lost sight of him, and he waved them over. "Come here, you guys." Then he continued in a heavily accented Spanish. "*Vengan, muchachos. Esto es increíble. Vengan a ver qué belleza.*" Everyone, not just the two bodyguards, gathered around him. "*Vengan, miren.* It's so good, guys." He removed his glasses to read the title, and then put them back on. "This is a terrific work. What do you think? *Mira, es fantástico.* 'Before the Future,' what a nice name. 'Antes del Futuro.' What does it mean? Don't tell me, I know. Of course, I know. 'Antes del Futuro.' What is the future? It is what you don't see. What is over there," and he pointed toward one end of the gallery. "What you don't see, what we don't know if we will see. That's it. Oh, boys . . . And this work is called 'Before the Future.' What is the before? That is the opposite of the future, it is what was over there," and he pointed to the other end of the gallery. "It's what has already happened. Oh, boys! If it's not the future and it can't be before, then, *¿qué es?* I know, I have an answer, *tengo la respuesta.* If it isn't tomorrow or yesterday, this work is today, the present, right now," and he pointed to the sculpture. "Here we are in the present, destroyed, rusted. That bent metal represents the

years, old age. The red represents childhood, when the mother
gave her child tomato juice. That blue next to the red, the child,
is the great sea. In other words, when we are children, we are
already condemned to come here by sea, to swim here. That
red child is Dominican . . . "

The gay man, smiling in amazement, interrupted him in
broken English. "Wa, why a Dominican?"

The man in the white hat touched the man's chin. "Well,
well, how nice that you understand Spanish, dear, because I
had a Dominican girlfriend. She was pregnant and fell down a
broken stairway, *sabes,* in the building where she lived. We
called a lawyer. And you know what? We lost the child and we
didn't get a single cent. We needed the child to get government
assistance, *sabes*, welfare. I lost the most, because she left me
and I was no one then, you dig?"

The gay man was agape. "What a fantastic story!"

Some of the people stood there in disbelief while others
dismissed the man in the white hat as a crazy eccentric.

"That red child is Dominican. He has to swim to get here."
From behind his glasses he searched for someone to assist him.
"I'll take my child. How much is it?"

The owner, solemn and serious, went over to him. "Ten
thousand dollars. You can pay . . ."

"No, no," he interrupted, "I'll pay right now. *Ahora
mismo.*"

The owner responded casually, "You can only take it when
the exhibition is over, so that others can appreciate it."

When he heard these words, Elías was about to cry out that

the exhibition was over. He was sure that any minute the buyer would change his mind. He made a superhuman effort not to flinch as he listened to the negotiations.

"No, no," the man in the white hat now spoke with a stern voice that did not welcome discussion. He motioned to the bodyguards to collect the sculpture. "Take the child to the limousine and put it in my seat. I will carry my child."

There was whispering, exclamations of surprise and mischievous smiles.

One bodyguard said to the other, "The boss is getting crazier every day."

"Just think, ten thousand dollars for this," the other replied.

"Who is the artist?"

"He must be around here somewhere."

"Son of a bitch was born lucky, huh?"

The man in the white hat disappeared with the gallery owner into another small room.

The gay man covered his mouth with his hand. "Wow! I can't believe it. *Ese* man *es un genio*. He's a genius. A genius in a white hat. Oh, God!"

A few people were congratulating Elías, and others congratulated Laura, for it was she who had organized the exhibition. Mario was flabbergasted. He shook his head from side to side and hugged Janeth so he could feel some solidarity, given what he had just witnessed. Elías had forgotten the entire discussion about modern art they had had in the bar. He was happy, for now he knew there was nothing to stop Helena from finally being by his side.

Janeth went over to congratulate Elías, and when she returned to Mario's side, he scolded her.

"Why are you such a hypocrite? How can you congratulate him for a bicycle handlebar?"

"That's not why I congratulated him. It was for the ten thousand dollars. Do you think it's not enough?"

They both laughed.

The Ticket Dance

If women really had a sixth sense, then the complicity between mother and daughter doubled it. Elías's poor five senses were outmatched by their twelve. Both Helena and her mother began to sense that Elías might not call again, which is why they tried to call him several times on the opening night of his exhibition, but there was no answer at area code 718. That very same night, Elías, Laura, Mario and Janeth went out to celebrate the sale of his 'Before the Future.' No one had expected him to sell anything, and certainly not for ten thousand dollars minus the agreed-upon twenty percent commission to the gallery. Even eight thousand was more than anyone could have imagined. Elías's euphoria was so great that he slept at Laura's apartment for the first time. They made love, and he didn't even think of Helena.

The day after the exhibition, Elías stayed home. His boss had given him the day off. He stayed home not just to recover from the excesses of the previous evening but to think about what to do with the money and how to put his life in order. He remembered what a great evening it had been and how beautiful Laura was, and he promised himself never to call Helena again. Not more than fifteen minutes had passed when the phone rang. The operator announced a collect call from Tegucigalpa, and he quickly accepted it.

The kindness of that voice took him back in time, as if he

had just been with her. He felt like a waterfall in a film that has stopped, as if frozen by a mechanical flaw, which is then fixed and begins to flow again. He fell back into the telephone's net that trapped him like a casting net traps a defenseless fish. As his condition that she not come through Miami was accepted without opposition, he did not hesitate to put the wheels in motion. She gave him the shortest period of time possible to allow for her visa application and the other minor travel arrangements.

When he hung up, he felt happily linked to his past. He thought of Laura and felt only a little sadness for what he had lived so intensely the night before. Between his guilt over Laura and his happiness over Helena's coming, happiness won out.

Helena again filled the house with song after the phone call. Overcome with curiosity, her mother interrupted the singing. "How did it go, Helenita?"

"It's all set!" Helena's face was not big enough to express so much joy. "It's all arranged, just the way we planned it. I have to call the night before I leave."

"What did he say?"

"He just gave me some advice for my trip. Like when I get to immigration, where they will check my passport, not to get in the line of any ugly women or men, or ones that are short, fat, freckled, or wearing thick glasses, things like that, or anyone of an ethnic minority, like the Chinese or blacks. He said that those people have complexes because of their ugliness or their ethnic group, and they take it out on foreigners. It's their only chance to feel important. It's the only power this life has given them. Do you think that's true? Could ugliness be the reason for people being so cruel?"

Her mother agreed. "Listen to him, he could be right. Most of those officers never smile. And what about the ticket?"

"He told me that in a few days a friend of his will bring me an envelope that will contain money so I can buy my ticket here, and more so I can show it at the embassy when I apply for my visa and also at the airport when I arrive, since he said that they ask you to prove you have money to live off while you are there. So next week I'll be receiving three thousand dollars in cash."

Her mother looked amazed. "How much?"

"You heard right. Three thousand dollars! He sold a sculpture for an amount that for us is a fortune."

Dina laughed as she had never laughed before and took her daughter by the arm laughing, dancing, and singing, "I want to live in America. Everything's free in America."

Miami International Airport

O h, God, what an airport, I must be dreaming. I'm finally in Miami. Ay, Ma, soon you'll be with me too. Let's see . . . No . . . That old lady looks very short and cranky . . . No, you won't be the one to stop me from entering Miami . . . That black man is tall and handsome, he looks like Mandela, well, I mean how he must have looked before they put him jail. I wonder why they put him in jail. You're a very handsome black man, but your line is very long and I'm dying to see Miami . . . This one with the potbelly and all the freckles, no, he looks like Archie, he won't let me in for anything in the world . . . That one, no, not that one, she looks like she needs a man. What a mess! Oh, my God . . . This one, wow, this one looks like a Latino Robert Redford from three decades ago . . . And his line isn't very long . . . Right here, this suitcase is getting heavy, anyway. That's it, my Redford, I'm staying with you.

It was the same officer who had let Elías in. "Next," he said, with his eyes glued to his computer.

Helena hesitated for a moment. "I've forgotten the little English I knew. What could 'next' mean? Why do they say 'next' to everyone? Maybe it's like López or Pérez in the United States. Everyone has it before or after."

The officer looked up at her and repeated "Next." She

guessed that it meant that the next person should go ahead, but she didn't dare approach the window.

The officer said, "Next . . . *Usted, señorita.*"

"*Sí, sí, gracias,*" she said, relieved that the man spoke Spanish.

"Your passport, please," the officer continued in Spanish, and he looked at the photo and compared it to Helena's face. He stared at her for a few seconds, and she became alarmed. "Your ticket."

"Ticket?" she said, pretending not to understand.

"Yes, to return to your country."

"I'm not going yet, I just got here."

"But you need a return ticket."

"I'll buy it when I return home."

"This was the airline's fault. They shouldn't have sold you a one-way ticket."

"Well, I told them I didn't need it. I'll go back by boat."

"Where are you headed?"

"Where else! Miami, of course. I'm going to stay here a few days and then go to New York."

"Miami is a big place."

"I know it is. Are you *mayamense*?"

"What?" The officer looked puzzled.

"Are you from Miami?"

The officer smiled. "Mayamense . . . Yes, I am."

"Does everyone speak Spanish here?"

"It's the first language. English is the second one."

Helena felt like she had a friend. "It's a very nice city, isn't it?"

"Yes, that's what they say. My mother loves it."

"So does mine."

"How many days do you plan to spend here?"

"I don't know. What would you recommend?"

The officer smiled again, confused. "Oh . . . I don't know. I'm the last person to give recommendations."

"Do you know the city well?"

"Sure. I told you, I'm from here."

"First you use *usted* with me, and now you are using the familiar *tú* form. Why is that?"

"I always use the *usted* form with ladies, and if I like them, I use the *tú* form."

"My mother told me that there was no chauvinism here."

The officer, rather than checking the passport, was studying her face, as if wanting to know all about her. "That's not chauvinism."

"What is it, then?"

"It's called being a gentleman, a *caballero*."

"Can I use the *tú* form with you?"

"I'd be flattered . . . "

" . . . And then you'll turn me away for having addressed an officer with the familiar form."

"Why would you think that? That's normal here. Many people I don't know use the *tú* form with me."

"No, it could be a trap."

"Trap . . . what for?"

"To not let someone in."

"No. I'm here to uphold the law, not to stop people from coming in."

"And what does the law say about me?"

"That your papers are in order, except for the ticket."

She opened her wallet and took out some money. "Couldn't you take a moment and buy it for me over there . . . ?"

The officer was taken aback and interrupted her, "What do you think, that this is my house? I'm working. How much money do you have?"

She opened her purse and took the bills out again.

"Okay, you don't have to show it to me. Do you have family in the United States?"

"No. By the way, can you recommend a hotel?"

"Is this your first time in Miami?"

"It's my first time out of my country."

"Is anyone expecting you here?"

"No, no one."

"Why did you come?"

"To travel. To see Miami."

"What were you thinking? Don't you know that it's dangerous to travel alone, without knowing anyone?"

"Miami, dangerous?"

"No, not just Miami, but any large city in the world is dangerous for a girl by herself."

"I think you're trying to frighten me so that when you don't let me in, I won't complain."

"I wouldn't do that to you. I like you."

"I like you, too. You seem like a nice person, even though they say that those who work for immigration . . . "

He became defensive. "Those who work for immigration what?"

"Well, they say . . ."

"What do they say?"

"That there's a requirement they have to fulfill."

"What requirement?"

"Not knowing how to smile."

He thought she was going to accuse him of something much worse, and so he smiled, relieved. "Now you see they do. We're not all alike."

"But most . . . "

"Have you had a bad experience?"

"No, I just told you that this is the first time I've left my country. I know because that's what they say everywhere, and it's even on the news."

"The news isn't always true."

"I know. Anyway, you seem nice."

"I am. Look, let's make a deal. I can't recommend a hotel or anything now because I'm working, and look at the line of people waiting. Why don't you take a taxi to this address that I'm going to jot down for you. It's a good restaurant in a safe neighborhood. Order whatever you want, and I'll pay when I get there. How does that sound?"

"Great, I don't know anyone. I really appreciate it."

The officer smiled as he stamped the passport. "Welcome to Miami. This means you are now in the United States."

She smiled back at him. "Now I can use the *tú* form with you."

The officer wanted to say something to make sure she would wait for him in the restaurant. He was over-excited and for a second he hesitated, but then he said, "You're very beautiful, and lots of people might want to talk to you, but be careful. Not everyone is nice like me."

"All right, officer, what do I tell the taxi driver?"

"Nothing. Just give him the address. It won't cost more than twenty dollars. So, can you wait three hours for me, or a little longer until my shift ends?"

"I don't know anyone, and I wouldn't know what to do. I'm not going to miss the chance to have a *mayamense* guide. I'll be waiting for you."

John F. Kennedy Airport

That night at John F. Kennedy Airport in New York, Elías ran like a bullfighter who has lost his cape from one screen to another, checking the flight arrivals, asking again and again at the airline counter, giving Helena's name with the insistence of a preacher giving the good news about Jesus to an atheist. Two months had passed since the night his life had begun to take a course that he was unable to stop.

He began to feel that it was all over, that he had been a victim of his own obsession and that the raft was deflating and the only thing within reach was a life preserver that, despite his efforts to grab it, was being dragged off by the violent waves unleashed by the storm. Laura, his life preserver, was drifting farther and farther away from the raft. The crew member feared his loss of control.

At first he came up with several explanations to justify Helena's not arriving: a change in dates, a denial of her visa, the pain of separating from her mother. He called Tegucigalpa. The telephone cried out like a shipwreck in the middle of a storm where no one would ever come to the rescue. It was almost two months later that Dina, Helena's mother, finally decided to pick up the phone. Elías was happy, but so short-lived was his happiness that it did not have time to register in his heart. Dina answered with an "Oh, it's you" capable of driving anyone to suicide. Then she immediately told him not to worry about Helenita, that she was fine and would be in touch with him soon. Then she added that if he had begun to forget her, that it would be wise for him to continue to do so until he had forgotten all about her. Then she hung up.

Shipwrecked in Search
of a Life Preserver

After a week of heavy drinking and the sporadic scolding of Mario, who was practically living with Janeth, he decided to see Laura again, not as co-workers who barely said hello, as had been the case since the day he had told her Helena was coming, but as part of a couple who sense that life was offering them an avenue for reconciliation.

He invited her to a Japanese restaurant. Maybe the age-old recipes of the Japanese would provide them with essences to stimulate the chemistry between couples who were in love but for some reason had grown apart. After an hour, he realized that the Japanese had lost the battle with Laura. She barely said a word, staring down at the tablecloth sadly. On the other hand, she could have left if she had wanted to. The fact that she stayed meant that, despite everything, she wanted to be there. It was hard for Elías to decipher Laura's sadness. She was fluctuating between reality and make-believe. After all, she wasn't the first or the only woman with that special ability to become gravely sad with the sole purpose of causing her partner to sink into the well of guilt, forcing him to surrender and ask over and over again for forgiveness, getting down on his knees asking for mercy, imploring for amnesty—in short, begging so that his deception would not appear in the annual report of the Committee on Human Rights. No one, not even the most naïve of readers, could believe Laura's sad act, since she had appeared as capable of loving him as giving him up if Helena were to come. Most people don't believe that that kind of ambiguity can exist in matters of love. That's why Elías's intuition told him that he shouldn't completely fall for her sadness. But since no one has managed to define love for certain, the window remained wide open to the possibility that Laura's sadness in the Japanese restaurant was real.

Elías did not say much until the first bottle of wine was almost empty. Without knowing how, he told her he was sorry, that he really liked her, and that at times even thought he loved her. Laura could not believe that was true, given that only days earlier Elías's face had lit up and his joy had appeared endless, and even his ability to speak English had improved noticeably with the news of Helena's arrival date. Neither Laura nor anyone would believe such a sudden turnaround.

Human beings tend to think of love as a slow process. There are couples who begin to really fall in love after a ten-year romance. Love has that extraordinary, mutant capability that can be confused with desire, affinity, admiration, the simple fact of liking each other, and so many other things that risk being confused with true love.

Neither Laura nor Elías believed each other, but something selfish must have given them the energy to pretend to believe each other. He told her again that he loved her. She took his hand because intuitively she knew that it is through the hand that you can tell just how sincere someone is being. The hands are the voice's aid. With the help of hands, words usually say more and are more effective. If the mouth lies, the hands give it away. She realized that he was neither lying nor telling the truth because the hand she held in hers seemed more like a glove than a hand.

And so the hours went by, with few words spoken and their glasses continuously raised to their lips, to justify their silence. The time came to leave, and that evening, the only ones who profited were the Japanese.

If Love Were a Literary Category

Who would have recognized Mario, that loner, that rebel with or without a cause, that contradiction par excellence, who never took love nor life seriously? Maybe that was it: maybe by not taking life so seriously, he didn't contradict it. And life, more grateful than death (as it should be), rewarded him by taking him down the road that led to Janeth, to a love that, by its circumstances, was more about satisfying the flesh than anything else, but transformed slowly and surely into true love.

If love were given a literary category, it would have to be satire. Those who search seriously and steadfastly for the love of their lives almost always, as a rule, end up failing. They've considered everything methodically: how many children they will have, where they will live, where they will spend their honeymoon, where to go on vacations, and what to do on wedding anniversaries. The affectionate side is not overlooked, either: books or psychologists to avoid arguments, how to behave when their homes become poor imitations of paradise. At first glance, a couple like that appears destined to be together forever and ever. But suddenly a difference in method can bring it all crashing down just as quickly as a great earthquake destroys a city. It all collapses, like a curse for having calculated everything, like a confirmation that such methodical planning serves only to challenge destiny, like ridiculing the roads of life. Only ashes remain. People ask how a marriage like that could crumble so easily. Love probably did exist, except without a strong foundation on which to build. A love of calculations that neglected to calculate that, as the years went by, the building needed new floors, and the fragile foundation was not strong enough to maintain its balance against the force of gravity. That would be a great satire of love, if love were a literary category.

On the other hand, some couples, like Mario and Janeth, are born from nothing. They wrap themselves up in each other without the eagerness to reach some goal but rather to have each other like allied armies, more allies than friends, united by a cause that, in the case of couples, is to fight loneliness. But some go beyond this, as in the case of Mario and Janeth, because they do not even come together to fight loneliness. Because although they were alone, they were so used to it that they were not aware they were alone. It was not until they began living together that they looked at themselves and discovered that they had been alone before. They discovered their loneliness when they no longer had it, which is why they did not suffer from it. Without knowing or even suspecting they were doing so, they began to build from nothing. Just by discovering they were alone and, with the magic of finding each other, they weren't alone anymore. From there, from deep within, without even knowing or sensing it, they were laying the foundation upon which they could build solidly, without rushing or hesitation, without desperation or patience, but by simply being together, without the sacrifice or the sweat that accompanies the poorly rewarded job of construction.

Mario and Janeth were a happy couple, so happy, in fact, that they did not realize at what point they had reached that state. Looking at them, one might mistakenly think they had not been together long, when, in reality, their lives were joined for eternity. In this, too, love is satire.

The Unforgettable Advice of O. Henry

"So they say that the husband is the last to find out," Elías said, sitting on the only bed in the apartment.

Mario was shining his shoes, rubbing the brush back and forth, convinced that he could make them even shinier. "Maybe she wasn't right for you."

"Just think . . . I was desperate, and the son of a . . . ."

"Forget about it. It's been three months. You can't talk about her forever. Latinos. Those Latinos are very passionate."

Elías poured himself a whisky from a bottle that had just been opened, and then he poured one for Mario. "So Janeth is making you renounce your Latin roots. Why is it that we Latinos have all the qualities that are assumed to be defects? We are drunk, noisy, passionate chauvinists. Is passion bad? Maybe not, if it was bad, what would that say about the passion of Christ? And to all appearances, Christ wasn't Latino. I think it's good; it allows artists to create. If not, how do you explain the works of Shakespeare, Van Gogh's ear, Edgar Allen Poe's suicide—and none of them were Latino."

"You're right. Who could be more chauvinistic than Othello? I think we Latinos have to start a world movement against the labels put on us. Why don't they say we are good fathers and that we make sacrifices for the unity of our family?"

Elías smiled, satisfied. "Now we're talking. Then how can

you expect me to forget what Helena did to me? You know what? Another man would already have gotten on a flight to Miami in search of revenge. But I'm not like that."

Mario put his shoes down and picked up his drink. "It's better this way because you wouldn't achieve anything, and you could end up in jail or even dead. Anyway, Miami is a big place, and even if you wanted to, you probably wouldn't find her."

"Of course, I would. I have her address. She sent it to me in the letter. Just think, she wasn't even worried about giving me her address. She definitely knows me well."

"Get rid of that letter. If I were you, I wouldn't even have opened it."

"Why not? I didn't want to have any more doubts, believing only what they said in Tegucigalpa, that her mother had already gone with her to Miami."

Mario tried to hide his laughter by taking a drink, but it was to no avail. "Sorry for laughing, but I couldn't help it. Those women played quite a trick on you. You can't deny they were pretty clever."

Elías downed the last of the whisky in his glass. "What an idiot I am. I deserved it. To send three thousand dollars! That tops it all. This could only happen to me. When you're an idiot in love, you go overboard. The truth is that I could have suspected almost anything, including that she might come through Miami, but it never crossed my mind that she would stay there."

"It's your own fault. Why didn't you ask for my advice? Why did you tell her to look for the best-looking officer? Especially knowing how beautiful she is, because in those photos you showed me . . . any guy in his right mind . . . Try to be a little objective. That officer let you in even when legally he should not have. How were you going to repay him? You've never even thought about it. So now you see, what goes around comes around, and the reward fell from the sky. It's just a pity that it was the woman you were waiting for. You were burned, bro."

"I know it's mostly my fault, but that's no reason for Helena to have done this to me."

"It wasn't Helena."

"Of course, it was the other one, that witch of a mother," he said almost hatefully.

Mario took a sip of whisky and savored it. "Not her, either."

Elías became indignant. "You're not trying to accuse me of hurting myself?"

"Not completely," Mario said, pausing to pour himself another drink, a pause that made Elías restless. "It was actually the city that took revenge on you. You shouldn't speak badly about any city, because cities have a life of their own, and they know who loves them and who is insulting them. Do you know where I learned that? It was a short story by O. Henry called 'The Voices of the City,' which is called 'Cómo nace un neoyorquino' in Spanish. That's what he said about cities, and that's why I love my New York, and whenever I can, I kiss her, say good morning to her, speak well of her, and defend her. Look, I've lived here almost seven years without suffering any tragedy or economic hardship. Thanks to my beautiful New York." He looked out the window and blew a kiss into the air. "Without you, I'd be a nobody."

"Do you have the book?"

"Yeah, the Spanish translation. Read it so it doesn't happen to you again. Besides, it's our duty to read O. Henry. He lived in our country. So, what do you think of New York?"

Elías defended himself. "No, no, no, never, I've never said a bad word to anyone about New York. It's fascinating. I love it."

Mario looked at him critically. "It's better to be honest. Cities can detect hypocrites easily."

"Why didn't you tell me that before? Maybe my attitude toward Miami would have been different. Maybe you and O. Henry are right. Just look, Helena and her mother went around praising Miami, and she found a husband right at the airport. They say he's very good . . . ."

". . . If he let you in," Mario said ironically. "Besides, you can't complain about your luck. This city has treated you well. Remember the ten thousand dollars from the bicycle handlebars."

Elías opened the refrigerator and took out some ice. "Which wound up being five thousand after what I gave to the gallery owner and Helena."

Mario shrugged. "Come on, you found it in the garbage."

"I sold a work of art," Elías responded, disheartened.

"Elías . . . "

"He saw something, that's why he bought it. Maybe there is no such thing as art. You just have to give shape to whatever it is, and the human being gives it its own interpretation. Maybe there is no art, only pretexts. We create the pretext that the human being needs in order to think. Maybe they don't even think, they just awaken something that lay dormant in their brains. Maybe art is the pretext for rejecting those ideas that human beings always had and didn't even know. Maybe we are only the cause, and the viewer is the effect, his own effect. Maybe we aren't artists but merely creators of pretexts."

Mario smiled, pleased. Without knowing it, he was the original for Elías, the original in bloom. Not when they had known each other in Tegucigalpa nor in the months in which they had lived together had he heard Elías reflect on things in such an iconoclastic way, and he admired it. "It could be . . . Art is indefinable. It might be exactly the way you just said. Maybe in the future, art will be completely different. You'll be invited to an exhibition of paintings, for example, and there will seem to be nothing, just empty walls, wine and cheese. Each viewer will have those empty walls at his disposal in order to create his own work of art, his own painting in his imagination. The preoccupation of the painter will then be getting someone to lend or rent empty spaces and placing titles on the apparently invisible paintings. Just imagine, it will be a state superior to the human being. I hope so, so that the sale of those handlebars isn't a fraud. Art is like cities: it doesn't like to be made fun of."

"Stop trying to scare me. You know I'm a hypochondriac."

Mario stirred the ice in his glass. "That's the word! Hy-po-chon-dri-ac, that's why Helena left you."

The peaceful look on Elías's face vanished, replaced by heartbreak. "It wasn't my fault. It must have been the immigration officer's uniform. Oh, what difference does it make now . . . but the letter, she should have never written to me."

Mario went over to the mirror and straightened the collar on his shirt. "Tear up that letter once and for all, and make a break with the past. There are so many intelligent, beautiful women here, like, well, Laura."

Elías searched for a folder on the small bookcase, opened it up, pulled out an envelope, and removed the letter.

"You're right. I'll do it right now. I'll read it one last time, and then I'll destroy it."

"Out loud and without crying." Mario smiled. "I want to hear it again."

Elías picked up the bottle of whisky and lifted it toward the light. It was just about half-empty. He poured Mario an extra big drink and then did the same for himself. They raised their glasses, clinking them together.

"This toast is for the final reading," he said solemnly. "Then I'm going to burn the letter," and he took a drink as if trying to drown himself. "It says . . . Miami, the day, month, year, and all that nonsense. Then it begins:

Dear Elías:

It must be quite a surprise, although not a pleasant one, to get this letter. I know what I did was wrong, leaving you there in the airport, waiting for me. I guess you must have thought the worst. I know because my mother told me you called, frantic. I'm sorry.

When I got to Miami, I thought about our relationship and realized that I have always really loved you like the brother I never had. So it wasn't really worth going to New York, when here I found the man I love. I love you, too, of course, but like I said, as a brother.

I told my husband you were a cousin of mine who lived in New York. He was happy and asked me to tell you to come visit whenever you want, either alone or with your girlfriend or wife.

Our house is your house. I told him you were my cousin, in case you had a problem with immigration; he would be able to help you then, give you advice. Besides, since his roots are Latin, he is jealous and a little macho, *but not too much. So, if I tell him about us, he would probably have you deported immediately. He's jealous, well, he's Cuban-American.*

You must think that I owe you three thousand dollars. I, too, thought so at first, and I was going to pay you, but then Mamá convinced me that men and women are from two opposing armies. You are a male soldier and I am a female one. You belong to the army my papá belonged to, and I belong to the same one as my mamá. Your comrade, my papá, deceived my mother by making her take her money out of the bank and then abandoning us. So I kept your money as revenge for what your comrade, my papá, did to my comrade, my mamá. In other words, we are even. Your army won one battle and now we won one. If you understand this, I know you won't be angry with me.

So, as a great soldier from our country once said, "Relentless in combat, generous in victory." Don't forget that you can count on me. Write to me, as my cousin, of course. My mother and I would be happy to hear from you.

Take care,

Helena

P.S. Mamá sends you kisses. And you know what? She's getting married. You have to come to Miami, O.K.?

Even if he had tried, Mario would not have been able to

contain the fit of laughter that overcame him, just as it had the first time he had heard the letter.

Elías, upset at Mario's reaction, half-smiled, looked at the letter and then back at Mario, who, restraining his laughter as best he could, said, "You should give me that letter. If I fail as a photographer, I'll become a novelist. I'll tell your story and include the letter, and I promise you I'll be a success."

Elías slowly began to tear the letter up into little pieces. "It's not funny."

Mario picked up his camera and got ready to take a picture. "Don't throw the letter out yet. You know what? When you finish tearing it up, stand up and throw the little pieces of paper into the air, like when the Argentine soccer team won the world championship for the first time. I'll take your photo."

Elías remained seated on the bed. "You're crazy! Stop joking around."

Mario's eyes and voice were not joking. "No, seriously, it will be a great photo, a historic photo."

"I'm not in the mood, man."

"It's not a matter of being in the mood or not. Besides, that doesn't show in the photo; the photo will show that you have been frustrated by that relationship for such a long time, and today, finally, you've broken with your past. It may seem absurd to you today, but in time, you'll like the idea and you'll have fun with it. Who knows? If the photo comes out well, I'll probably use it in an exhibition one day and call it 'The New Man.' What do you think?"

Despite Elías's grumbling, he was willing to agree to the request. "Okay."

"I'll tell you when . . . Now . . . Throw the papers . . . Throw them over your head . . . Wow! Fantastic! It's brilliant! This deserves another toast."

"I hope you aren't going to ask me to sweep the floor, too."

"No, no, I'll do that, don't worry. This photograph is a masterpiece because behind that letter, an entire history is hidden. It could be the same with your handlebars."

Elías tried to force a laugh. "So now you're justifying my sculpture made from junk? What do you know? We don't know the history of the bicycle. Maybe someone killed himself on it or maybe it saved someone's life, or maybe the bicycle ran someone over or was a gift from a girlfriend to her boyfriend, who then got killed by a car when he was taking it for his first ride. Then it wouldn't be a very nice history."

Nothing or nobody was going to deflate Mario's optimism. "Could be, but it sounds corny. Maybe the bicycle belonged to a Chinaman or a Mexican who worked in a restaurant in Manhattan and used it to make deliveries, and someone from the Bronx stole it and then sold it, and the one who bought it had it stolen by someone from Harlem, who had it stolen by someone from Long Island, who went to sell it to the same Chinaman or Mexican from the restaurant in Manhattan, and then this guy had it stolen again, only this time by someone from Brooklyn . . . "

"Enough, what a ridiculous story," Elías interrupted. "What's the point?"

"To show that life is circular; everything is a circle around which we all rotate."

The sculptor became himself again and poured himself another drink. "Hey, a bit of brotherly advice, don't become a philosopher or they'll throw you off the Empire State Building."

"It's just that I'm in shock. I had given up hope that you would make a break with the past."

"What was left? Helena got married practically overnight, and even the old lady, Helena's mother, is getting married in Miami."

Mario raised his glass as if making a toast. "Great! You should be happy. I told you life was circular, right? Now it's the old lady's turn to suffer because she's going to marry a neurotic old guy."

"How do you know?"

"I don't know. It's just a feeling I have. In Miami there are lot of neurotic old men."

"There may also be old men who aren't neurotic."

"Those are already married."

"That's it," Elías said excitedly. "When the old lady gets married, she's going to pass her neurosis on to the old guy."

Mario was pensive. "I hadn't thought of that. I'm sorry, my brother, right now life isn't giving you the opportunity for revenge."

He smiled sadly. "I don't have the right to seek revenge. I was her revenge for what Helena's father did."

"Why you? What did you have to do with that? You said yourself that you had never even seen a picture of him."

Elías took a sip of his drink. "That's the problem. I don't know. Maybe you're right, maybe life is circular. Who knows, the old lady's theory about the male soldier and the female soldier may not be so crazy, after all."

"Well, there's nothing you can do but move on."

The sculptor sighed. "Yeah, I feel like a veteran."

"Cut it out. You're going to make me cry."

Elías's face suddenly changed, as if a dark road had just been illuminated. "Hey, if you marry a woman who has Latin parents but was born here, can you get a green card?"

"Sure."

"If you aren't in love when you get married, can the judge tell, can he see it in your eyes?"

"I don't think so. Judges don't look for that. And even if they could tell, there are many cases of couples who get married for the work papers and they end up falling in love. You just never know."

"How much will a suit cost?"

Mario opened his closet. "Look, brand new, it's yours. You can get married in it as many times as you want. Let's talk on the way. I assume you're coming with me. I'm going to a party with Janeth and Laura. She shouldn't be alone, and I can't walk around with two beautiful women all by myself."

Traces of doubt appeared on Elías's face.

Mario insisted, "Don't be silly. Today you broke with yesterday, and we have to celebrate, and what better way than with us, I mean, with Laura? Go take a shower and get dressed, and don't drink anymore, because you're already half-drunk, and so am I."

Elías began to unbutton his shirt. "Hey, if you were to get married, I mean, if I were to get married and I asked you for advice as a friend, a brother, would you give it to me?"

Without realizing it, Elías had found his original from which he was slowly but surely moving away, leaving behind his condition as an original in bloom, as a pale copy.

"Without even asking, I'd give it to you. What's up?"

Mario responded.

"If you were to get married," he said, with a pause brought on by intoxication, "let's say, actually, if I were to get married, where would you recommend I spend the honeymoon? Outside of New York City, of course."

Mario thought it over for a few seconds. He looked over the titles on his small bookcase, pulled one out, and threw it on Elías's sleeping bag. Elías went over to find that it was a collection of short stories by O. Henry.

"It depends. Would you get married in the summer or the winter?"

"Hmmm . . . Maybe closer to winter."

Mario smiled maliciously. "Wait . . . Let's see what I can think of. You know what? It has to be a place that Laura likes, because she loves you and she told me she doesn't mind taking the risk. And if she said so, it's true, because I've known her for a long time. What would you think, say . . . of Miami?"

Also by Roberto Quesada

El desertor

El humano y la diosa

The Big Banana

The Ships (Los Barcos)

When the Road is Long, Even Slippers Feel Tight:

A Collection of Latin American Proverbs

(editor)